An I CAN READ Mystery

BINKY BROTHERS

AND THE

FEARLESS FOUR

by James Lawrence

Pictures by
Leonard Kessler

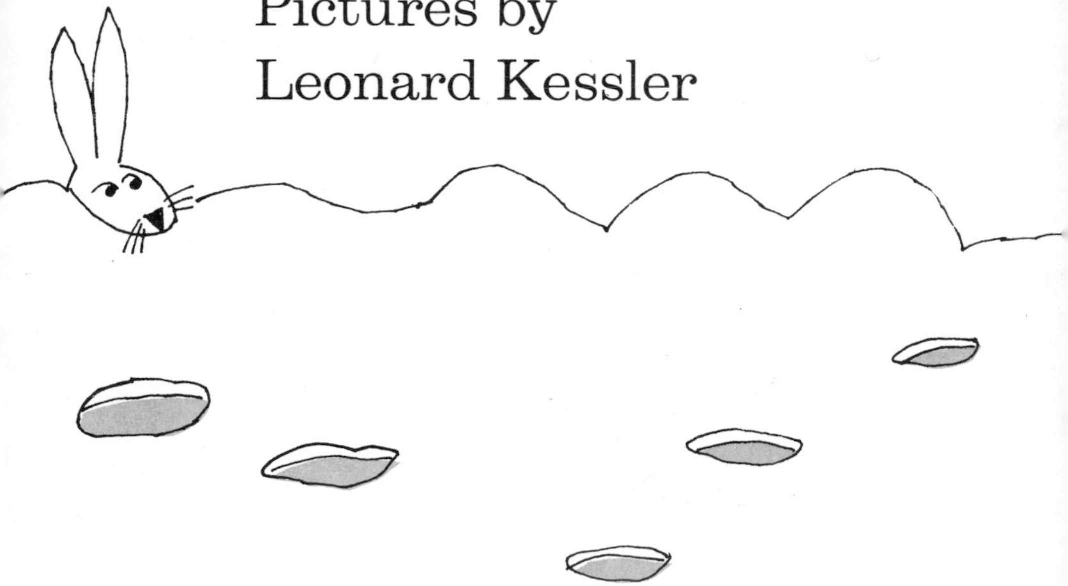

Harper & Row, Publishers
New York, Evanston, and London

For Sherry, Liane, Jim, John,
Vivian, and Gillian

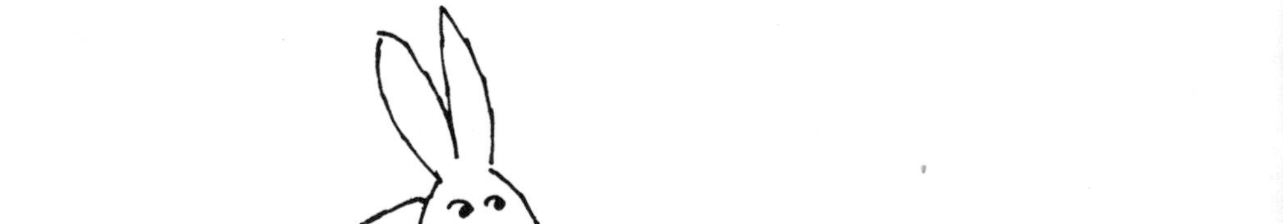

BINKY BROTHERS AND THE FEARLESS FOUR

 For information address Harper & Row, Publishers, Inc., 10 East 53rd Street, New York, N.Y. 10022. Published simultaneously in Canada by Fitzhenry & Whiteside Limited, Toronto.
Library of Congress Catalog Card Number: 75-77936

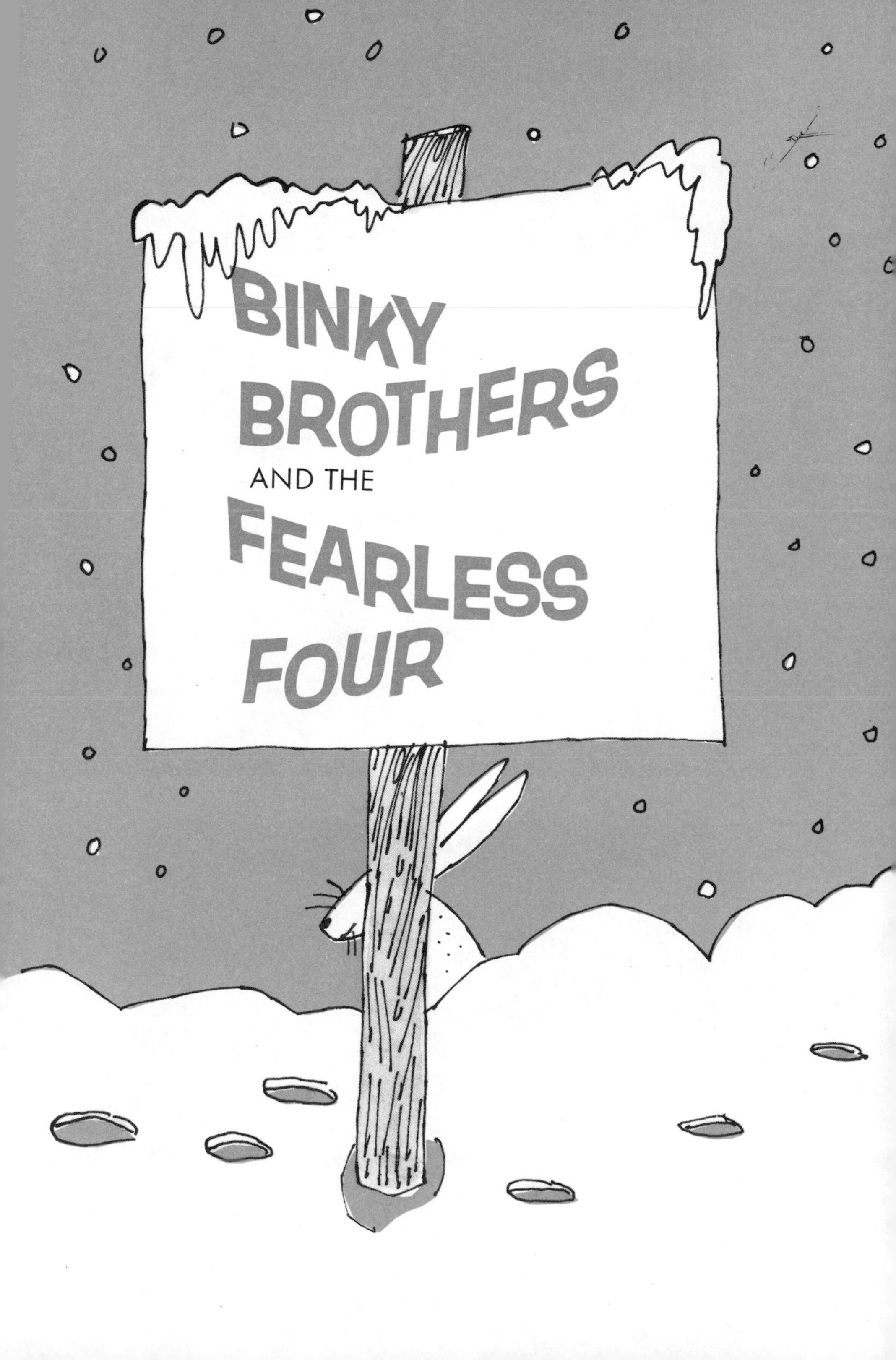
BINKY
BROTHERS
AND THE
FEARLESS
FOUR

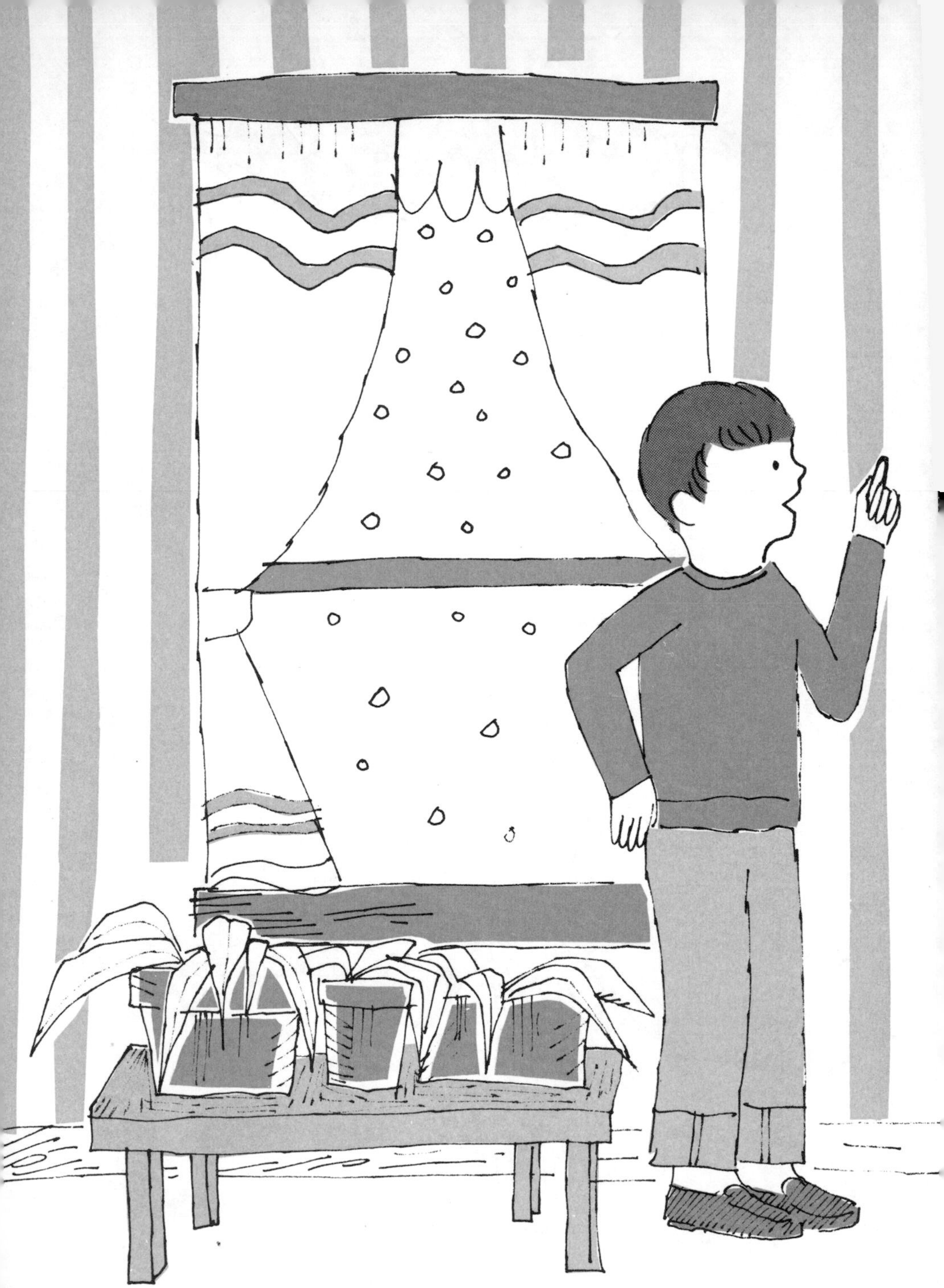

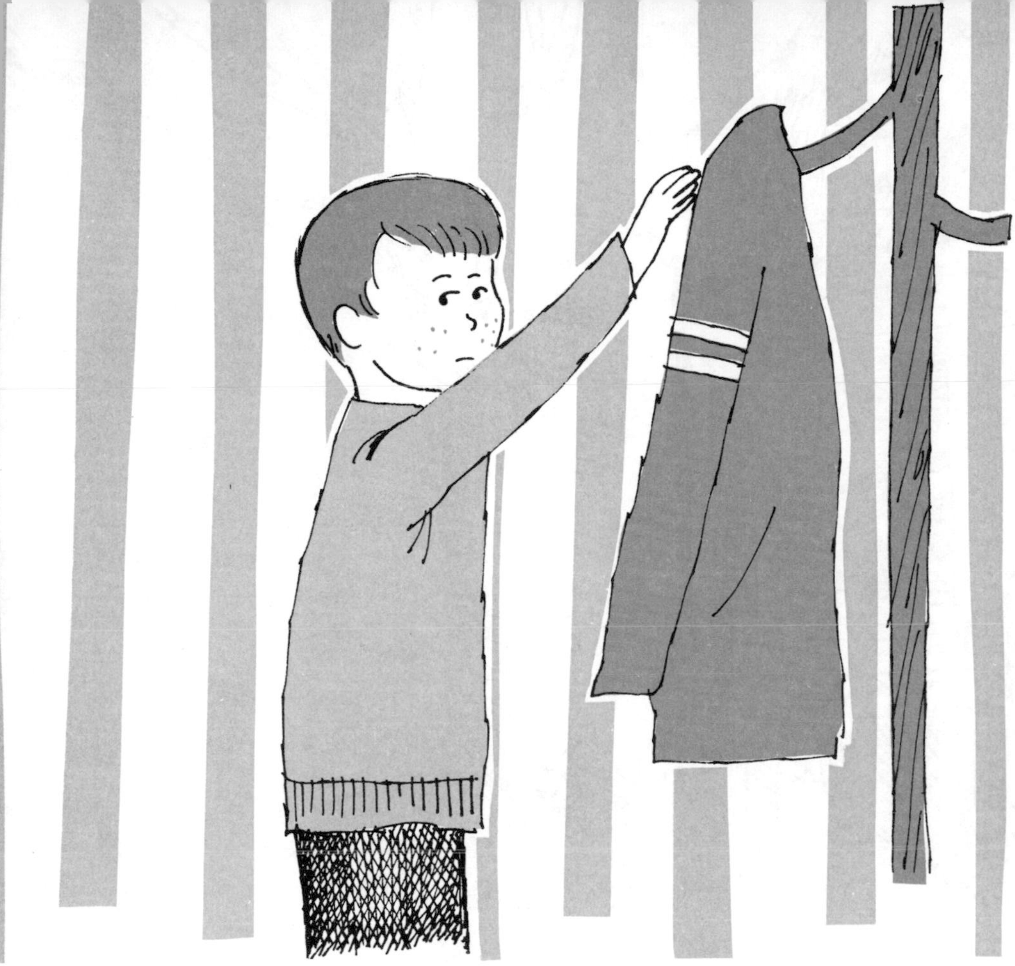

“Where are you going?”

Dinky asked his big brother.

“Out,” said Albert Binky.

The kids all called him Pinky Binky

because he had red hair.

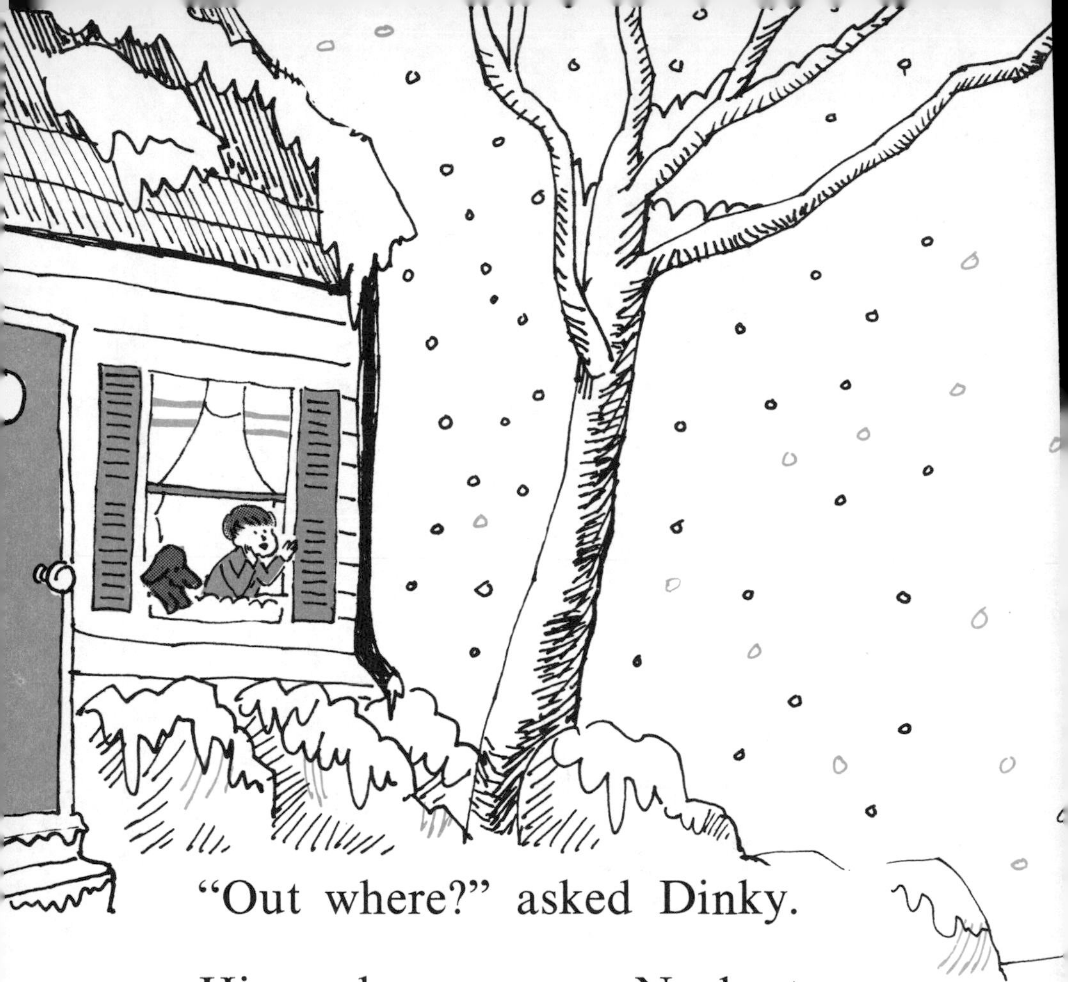

"Out where?" asked Dinky.

His real name was Norbert,

but Dinky fitted better.

"To meet the guys in my club,"

said Pinky.

"We are making a snow fort."

"Can I come?" asked Dinky.

"No," said Pinky.

"We are the Fearless Four.

We do important secret stuff.

You are too little

to be in our club."

"Oh, phooey," said Dinky.

The snow fort was half up.

"What about eats?" said Pinky.

"We will need food in our fort."

"Right here," said Chub Doolin.

He popped a jelly bean into his mouth.

A boy came along.

None of the Fearless Four knew him.

"What are you guys doing?" he asked.

"What does it look like?" said Mike.

"This is a top-secret hideout
for our club," said Pinky.

"We cannot talk about it."

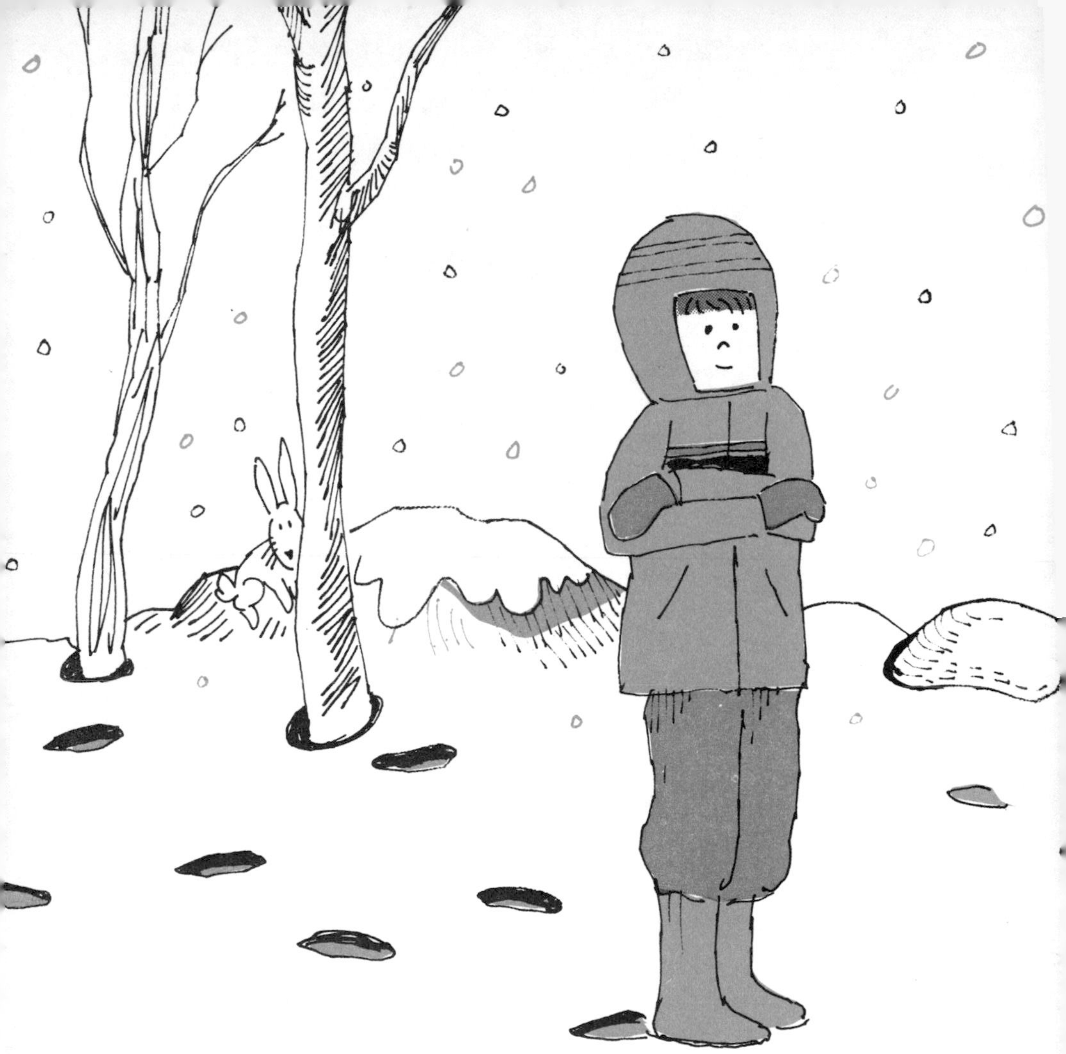

"I am Bob Green," said the boy.

"Can I be in your club?"

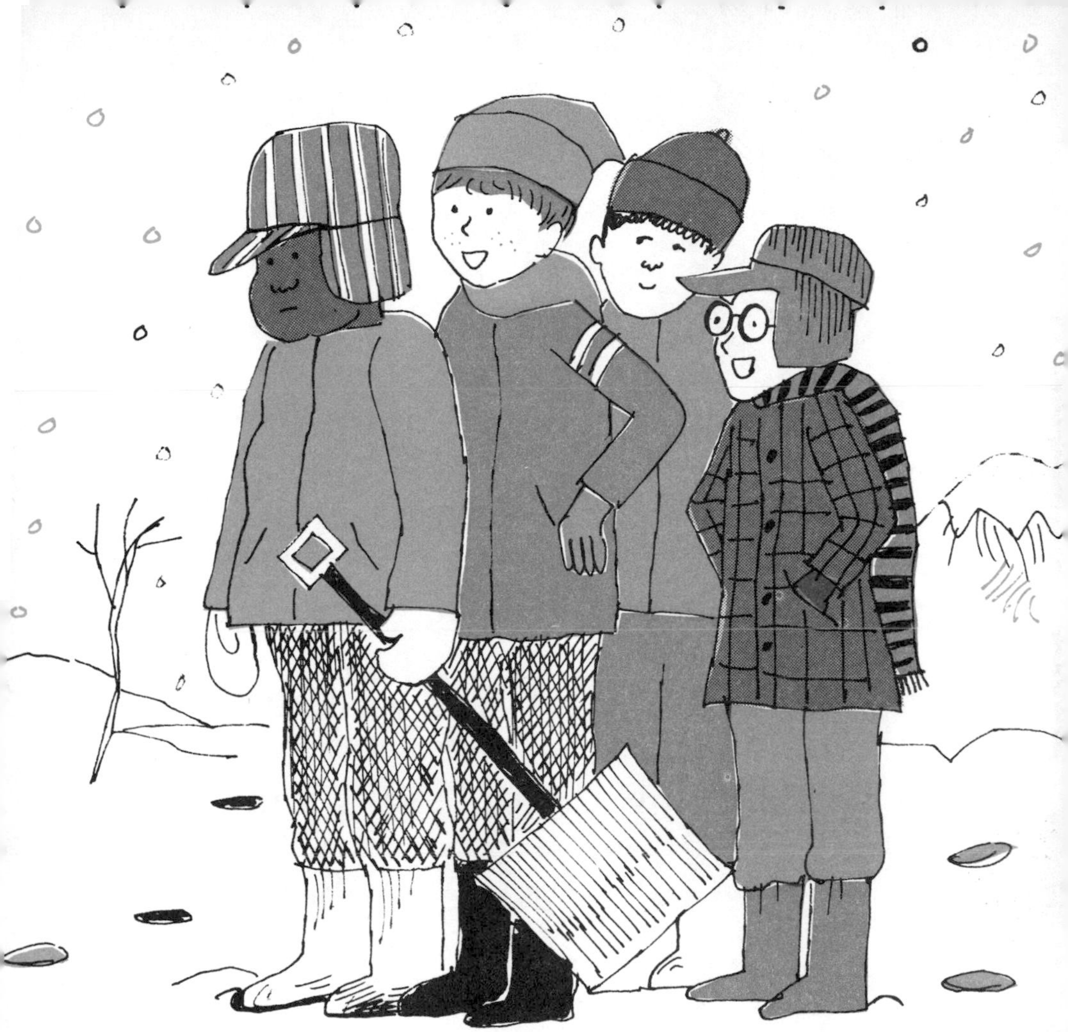

The Fearless Four did some whispering.

Then they shook their heads.

"Nope," said Pinky.

"We are the Fearless Four."

"If we let you in," said Spud,

"we would have to think up

a new name for our club."

"Can't you call it

the Fearless Five?" asked Bob.

"Nothing doing," said Pinky.

"Besides, you are probably

not fearless enough."

"I am so," said the new boy.

"You and your old club

better watch out!"

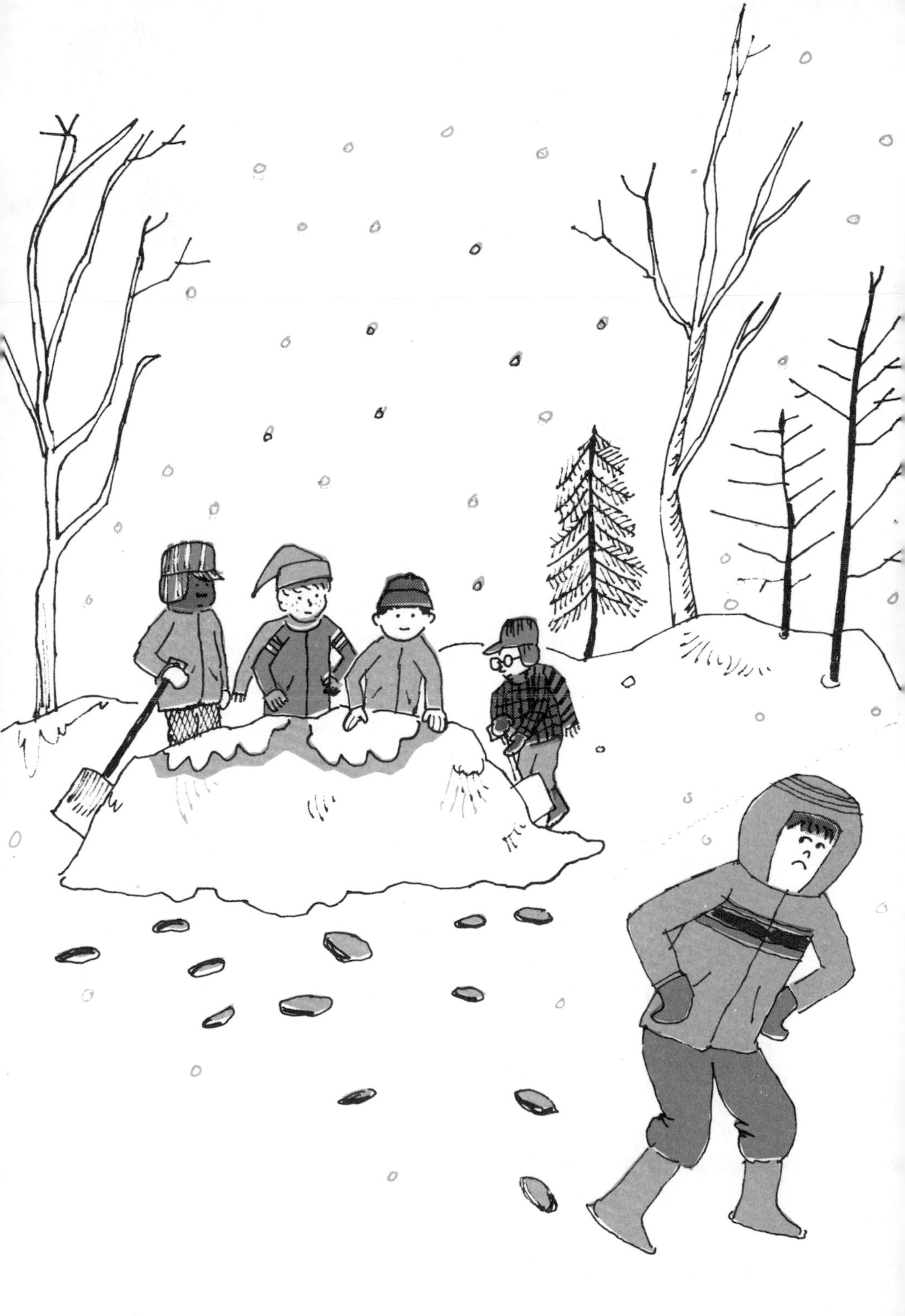

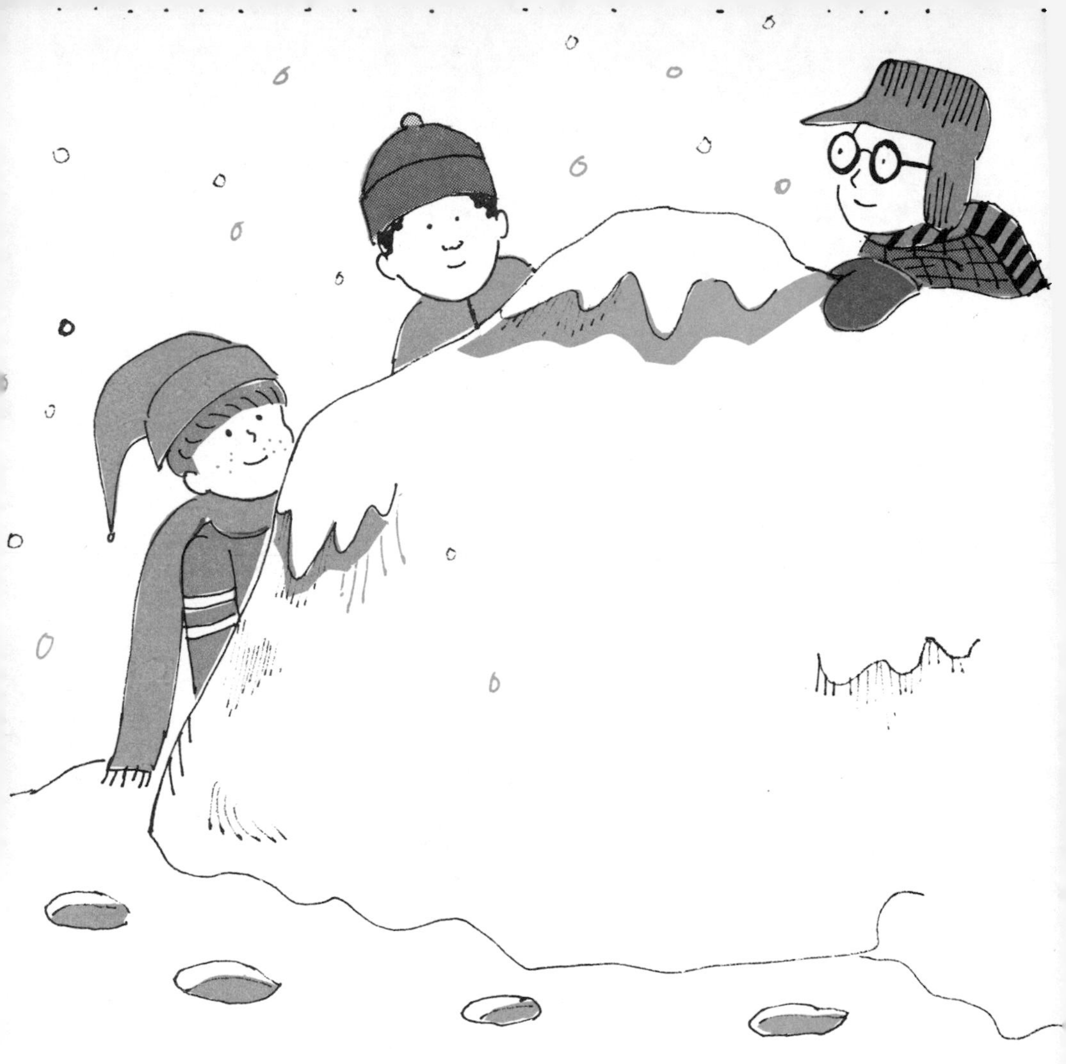

The Fearless Four worked
all afternoon.
They finished their snow fort.

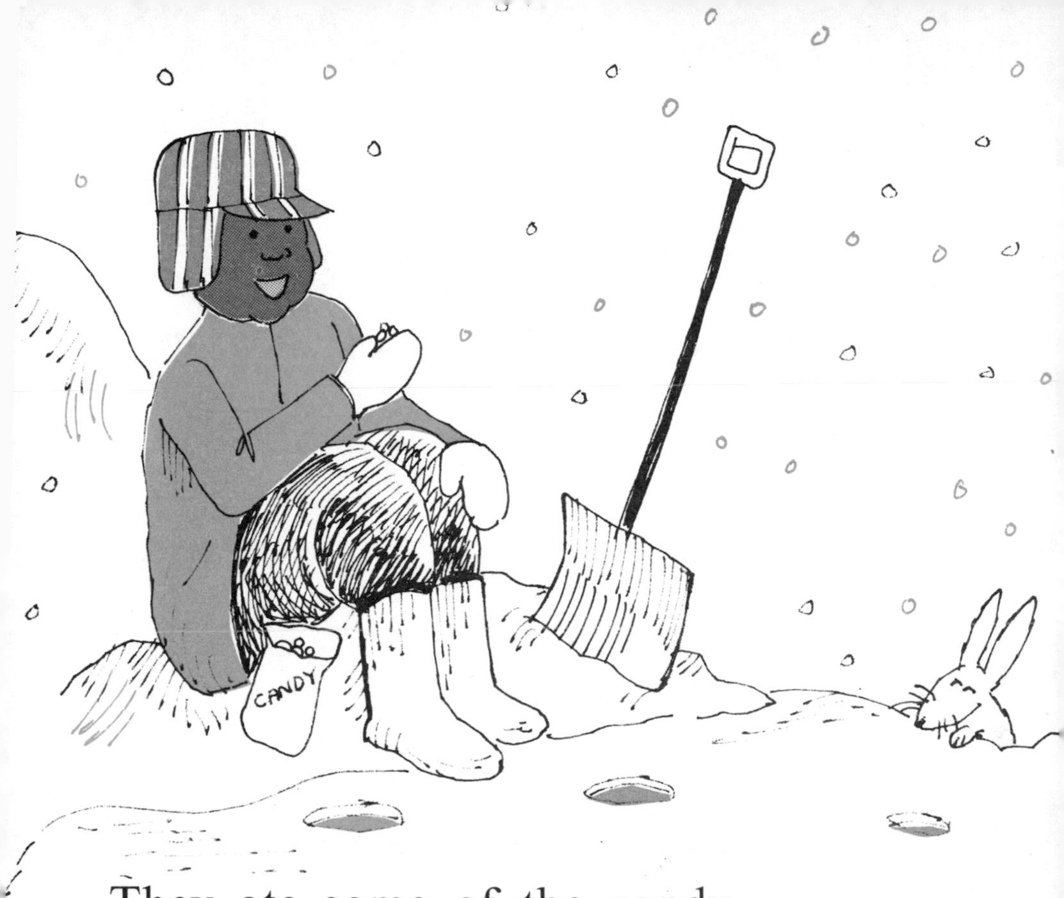
CANDY

They ate some of the candy.

Chub thought they should eat it all.

But Pinky said, "We better save some

in case of enemy attacks."

So they hid the rest of the candy

inside the fort.

Suddenly Mike gave a yell.

"Look what someone stuck in the snow!"

"Probably that new kid," said Spud.

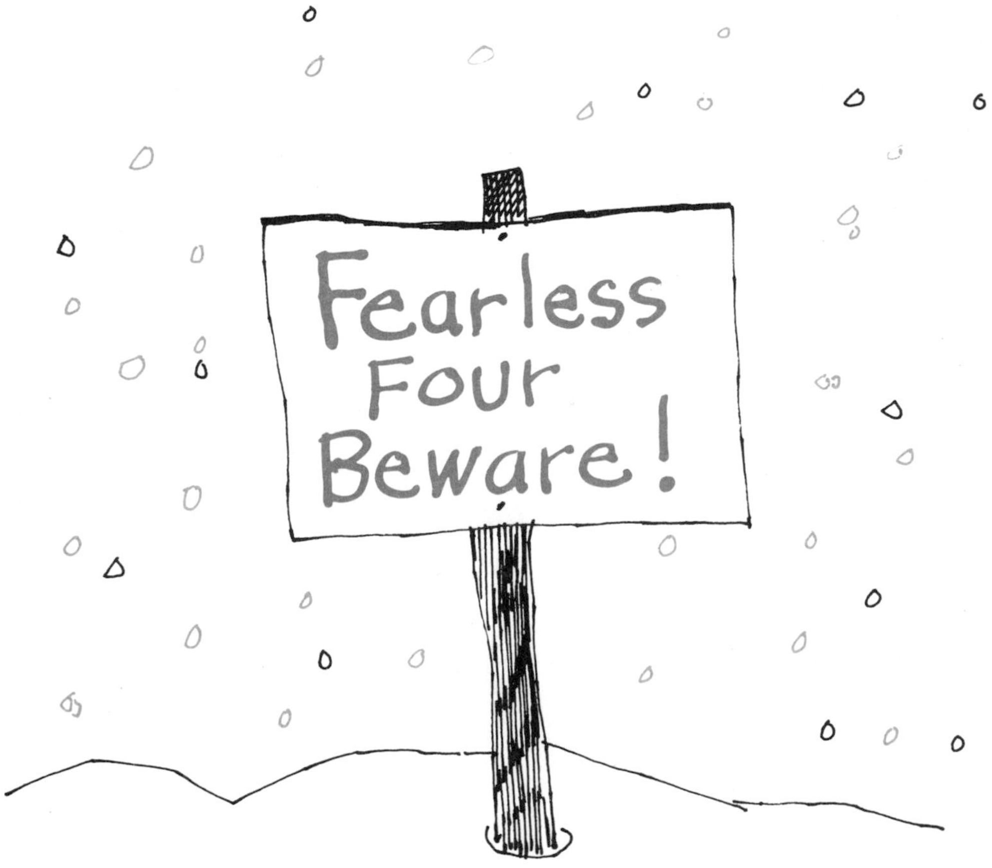
Fearless
Four
Beware!

"What should we do?" said Chub.

"You live closest," said Pinky.

"When it starts to get dark,

come back and watch."

Chub looked a little worried,

but he said, "Okay."

Pinky went home.

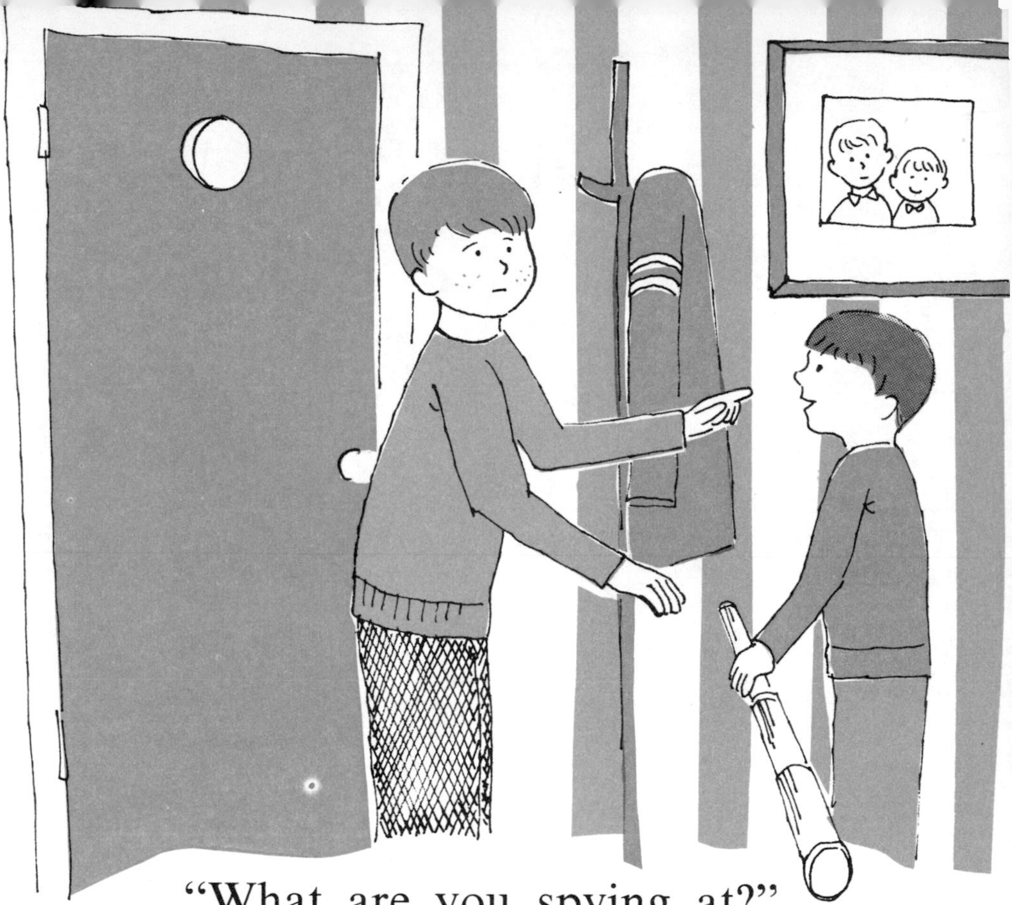

"What are you spying at?"

he asked his little brother.

"A new family is moving in

across the street," said Dinky.

"Don't be so nosy!" said Pinky.

"Give me that telescope!"

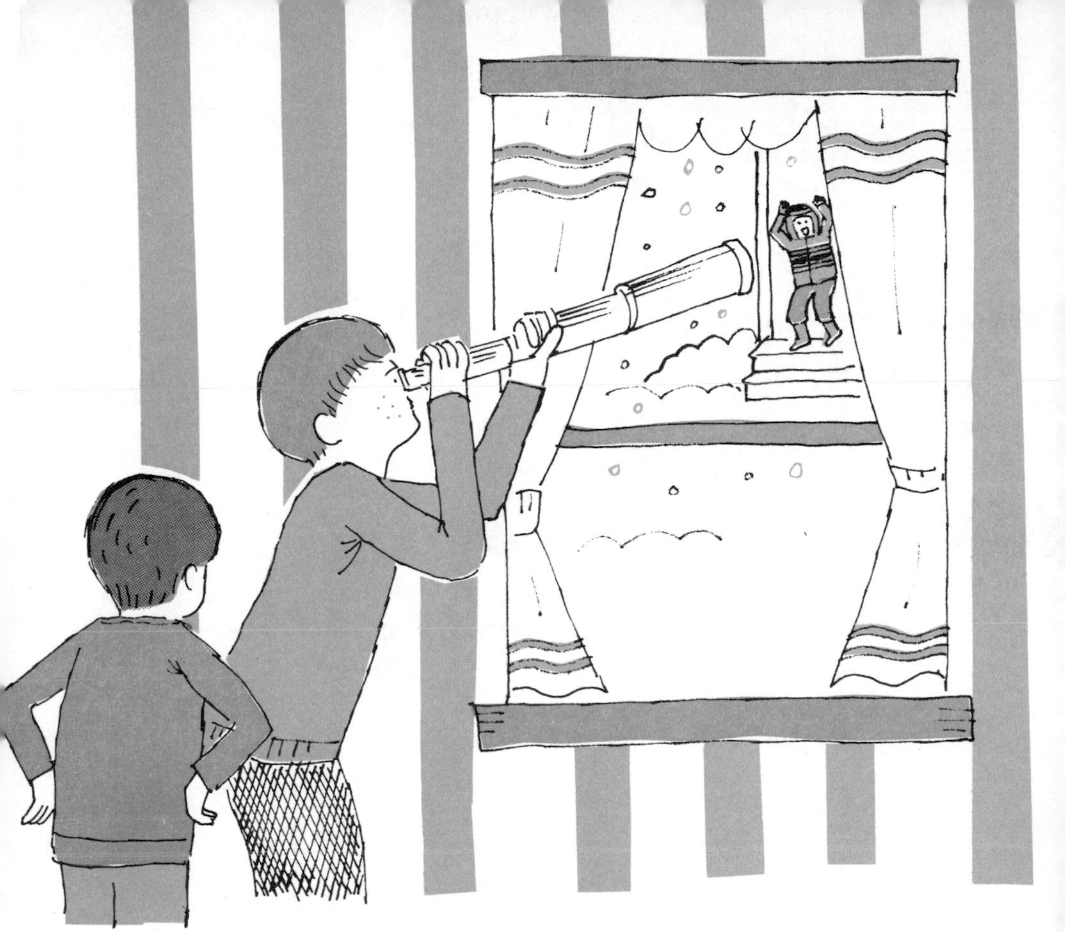

"It is that new kid," said Pinky.

"Bobby Green," said Dinky.

"I know," said Pinky.

"He came snooping around

our snow fort."

"Not Bobby," said Dinky.

"Yes, Bobby," said Pinky.

"And now the rat

is making faces at me."

Bobby hollered something

and ran into the house.

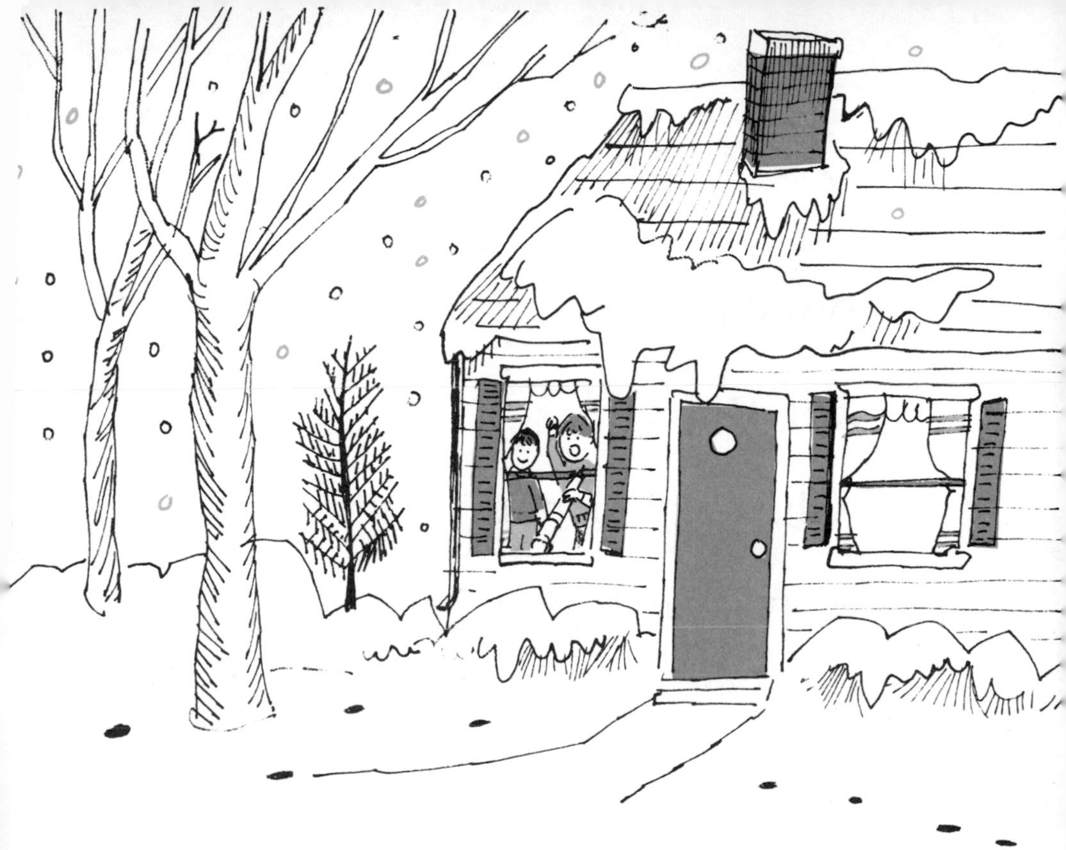

Pinky's face got red.

"It sounded like Nosy," said Dinky.

"I did not hear," said Pinky.

"That kid thinks he's smart.

I bet he is going to try

and raid our fort."

"You're wrong about Bobby,"
said Dinky.

"Oh, no, I'm not," said Pinky.

"I will catch him."

"How?" asked Dinky.

"That will be easy," said Pinky.

"I am one of the Fearless Four.

He knows I will be watching,

so he will duck out the back door.

But I will follow him."

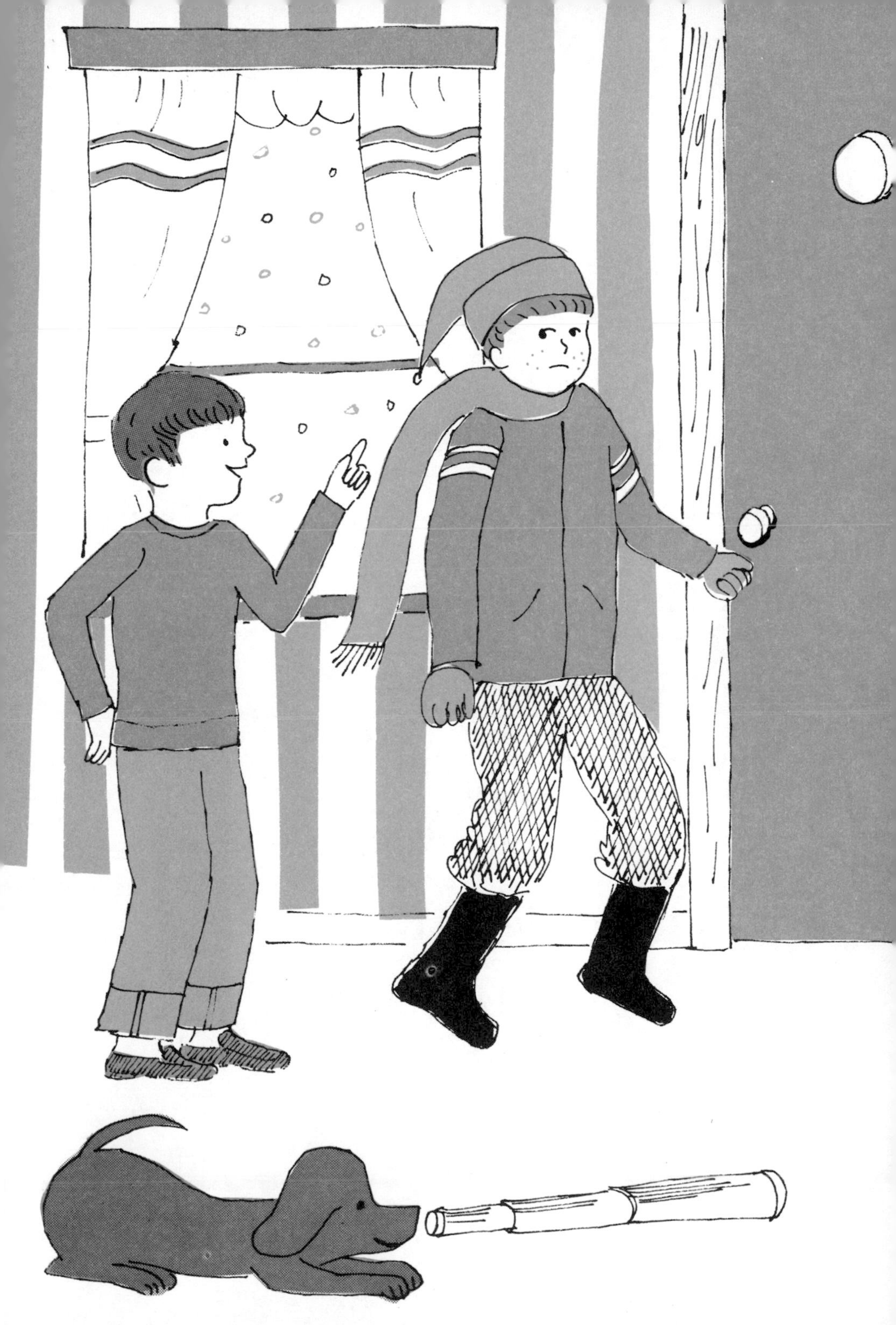

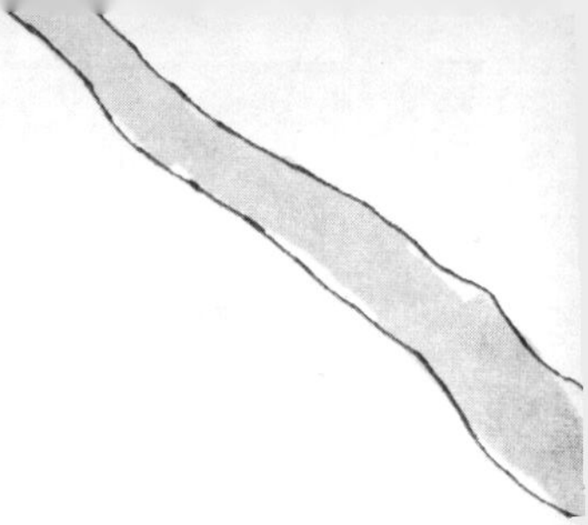

Pinky hurried around the block.
He tiptoed into the Greens' backyard
and hid in the bushes.
Ha ha, thought Pinky.
Now let him try and sneak out!
Pinky waited and waited.
It was cold out there,
just staying still in the bushes.

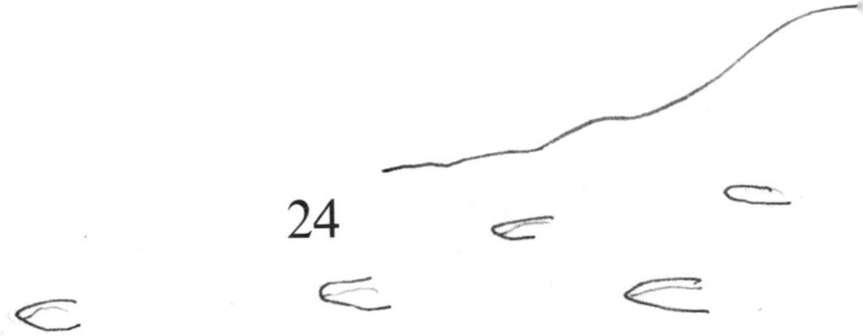

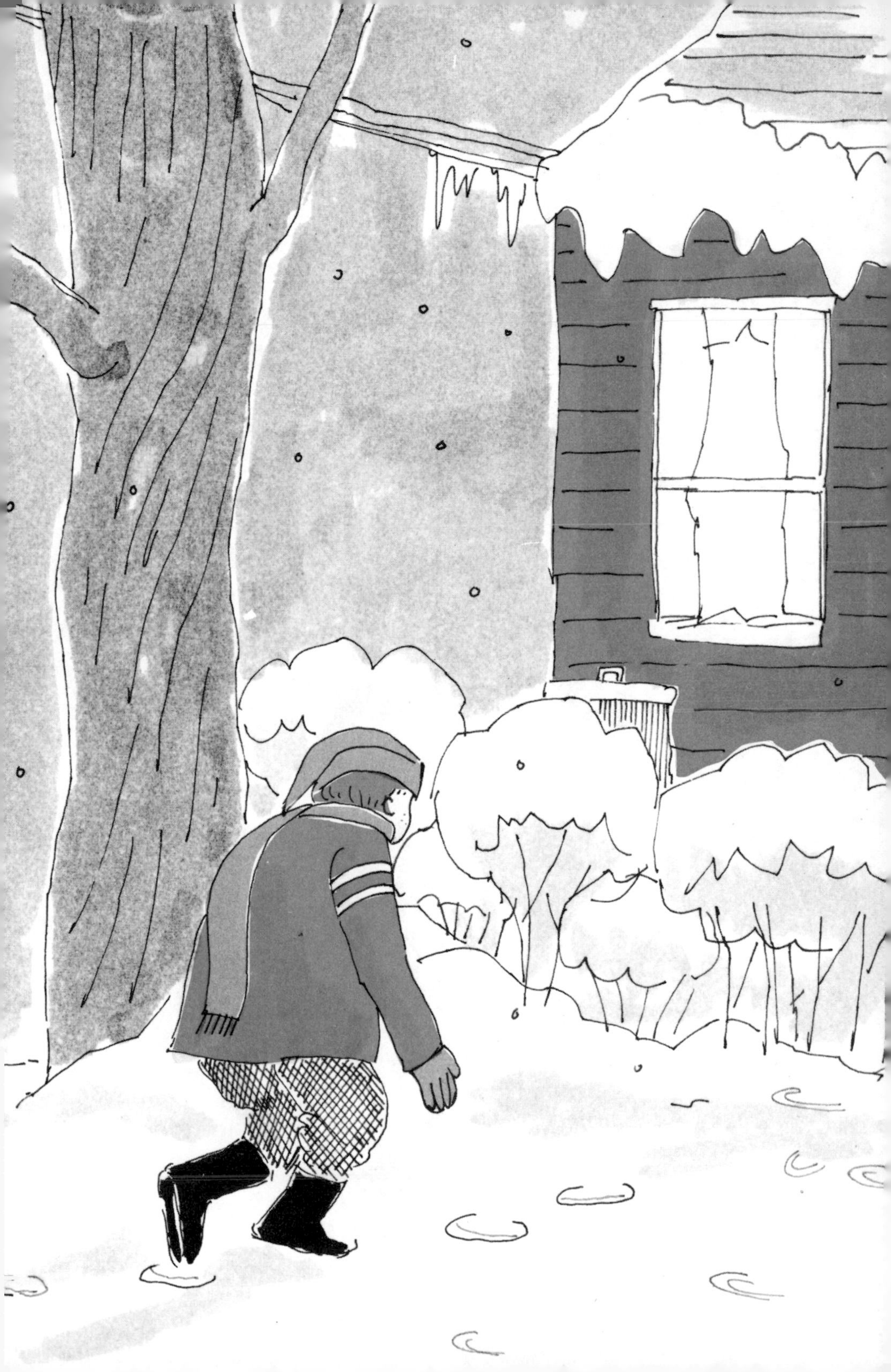

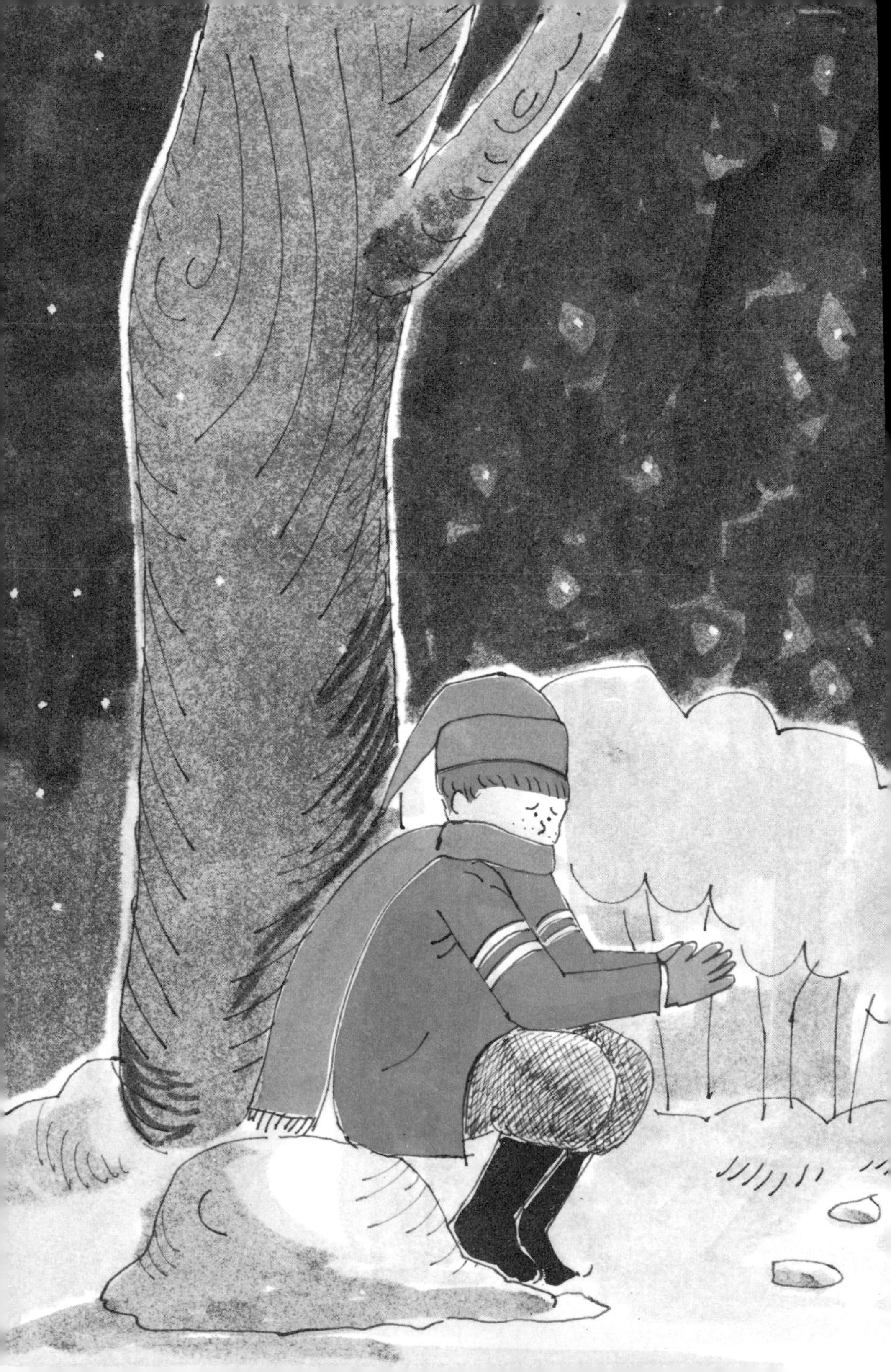

After a while it got dark too.

And spooky.

Pinky began to shiver.

"S-s-so what?" he said to himself.

"I am one of the Fearless Four.

Nothing scares me."

But he kept on shivering.

All of a sudden someone yelled,

"Hey, Pinky!"

Pinky almost jumped out of his skin.

That dumb brother of mine,

he thought.

"Shhh!" he said.

"They will hear you in the house.

Then Bobby will not come out."

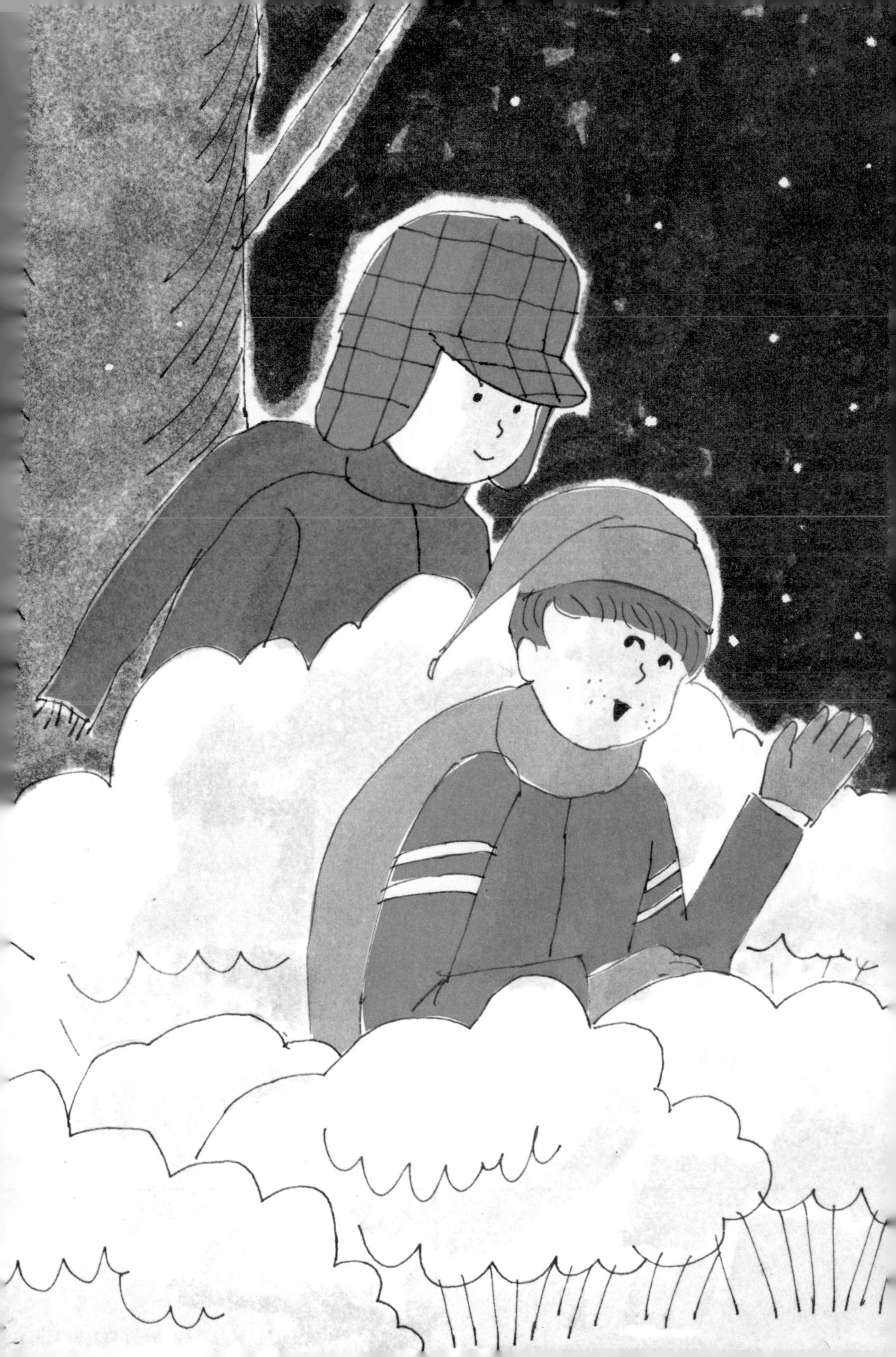

"You can stop watching," said Dinky.

"Bobby came out the front door

a long time ago."

Pinky peered up over the bushes.

He was so stiff

he could hardly stand up.

"Why are you hiding in our bushes?"

asked Bobby.

"Never mind why," Pinky growled.

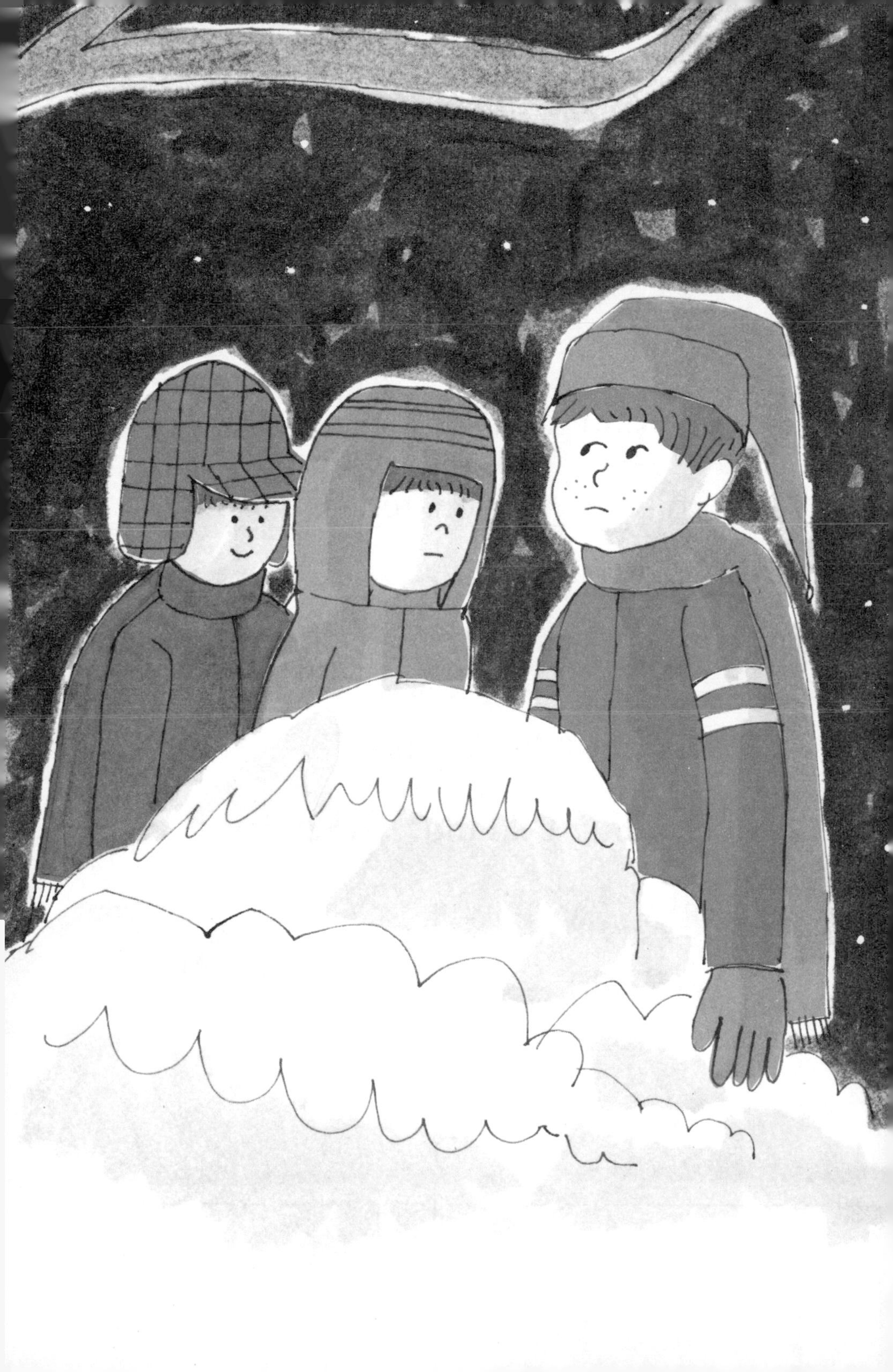

"Chub just called up," said Dinky.

"He said something awful happened.

A big hairy monster

wrecked your snow fort."

"A hairy monster?" said Pinky.

"He must be kidding."

"He didn't sound like it," said Dinky.

Pinky was mad.

And cold.

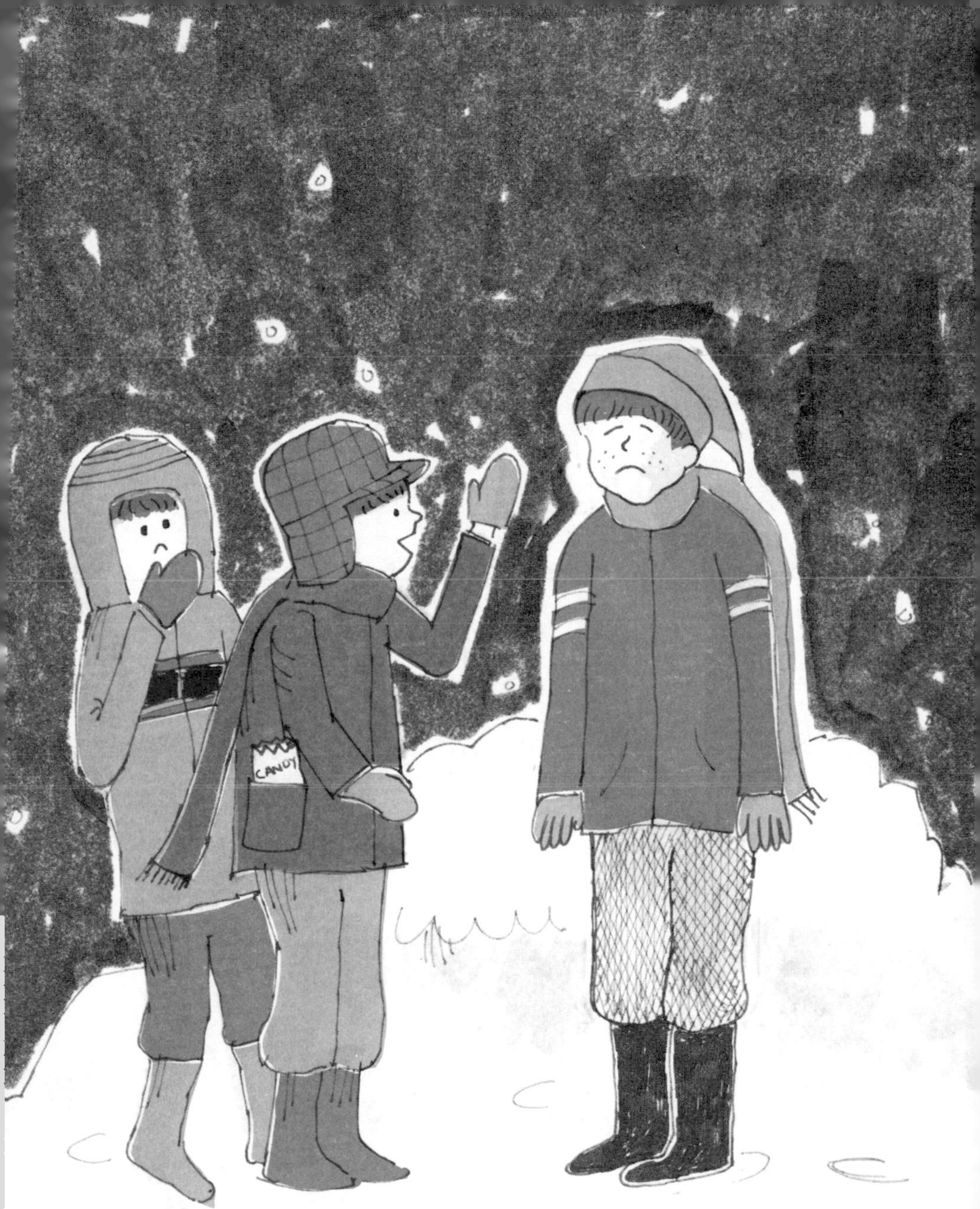
CANDY

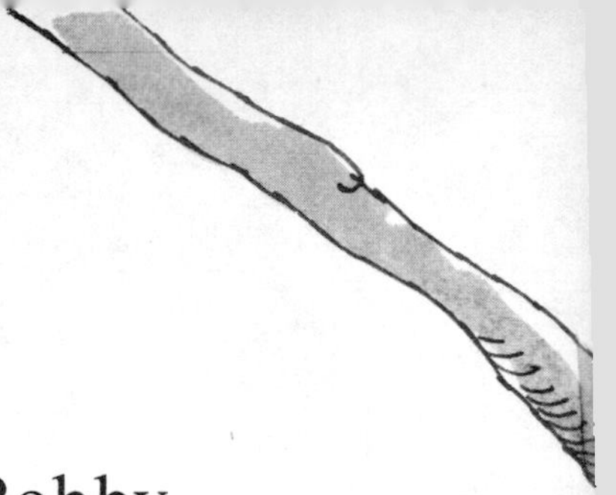

He looked hard at Bobby.
"Okay, wise guy.
What is the big idea,
wrecking our snow fort?"
"Don't look at me," said Bobby.
"I've been playing with Dinky
ever since I came out."
Pinky glared at his little brother.
"Why didn't you tell me?
I almost froze out here."

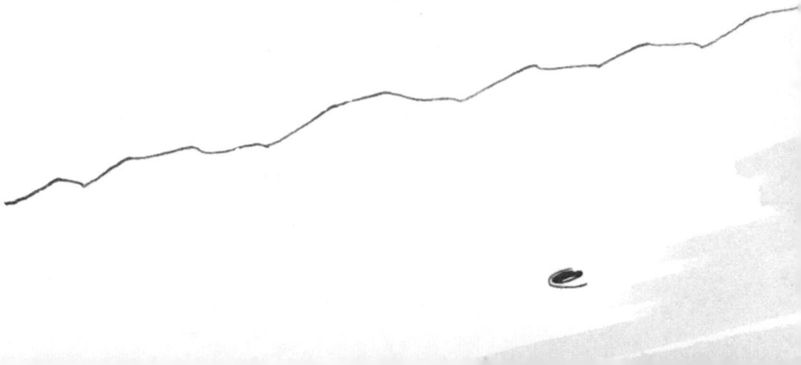

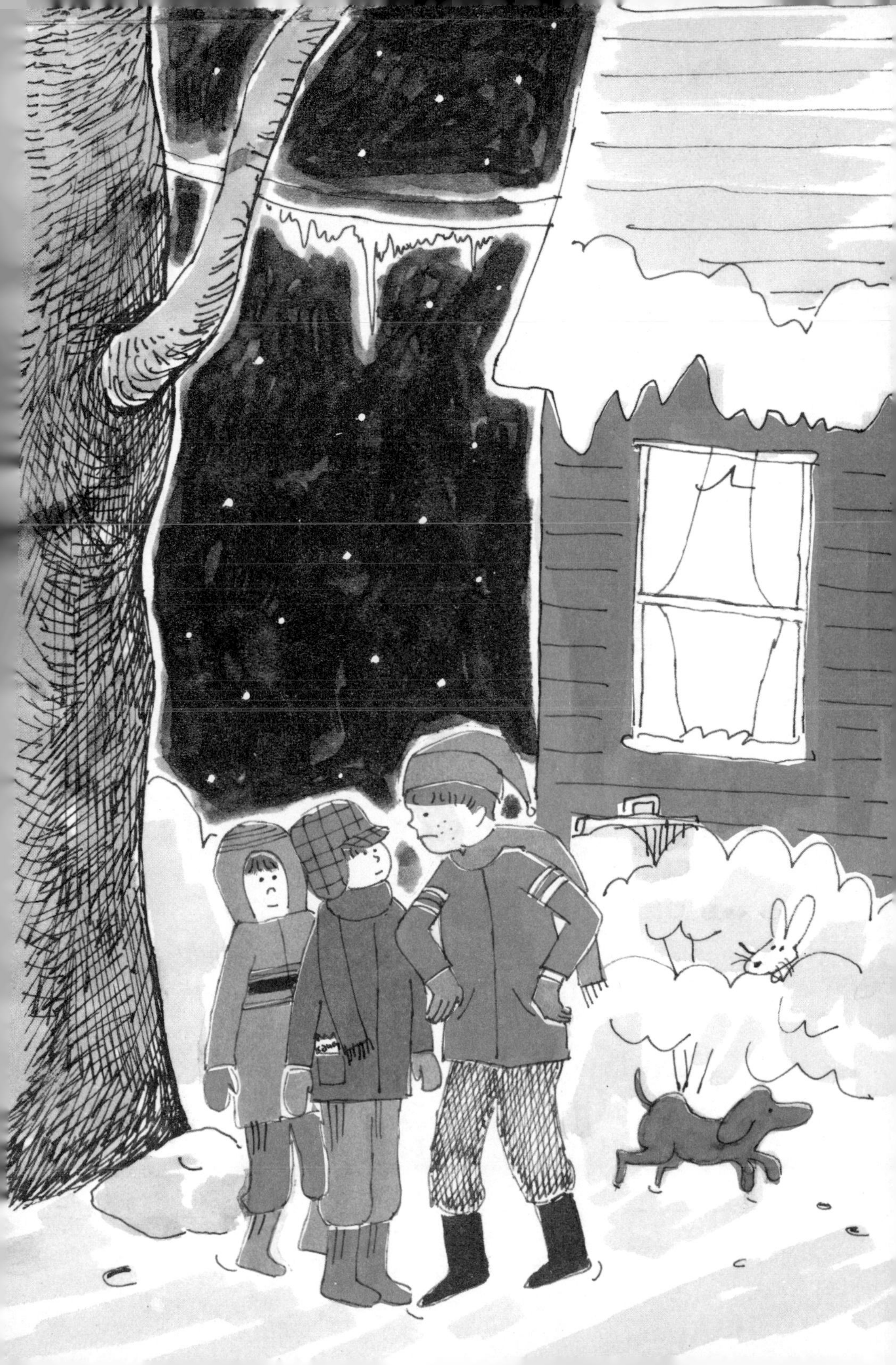

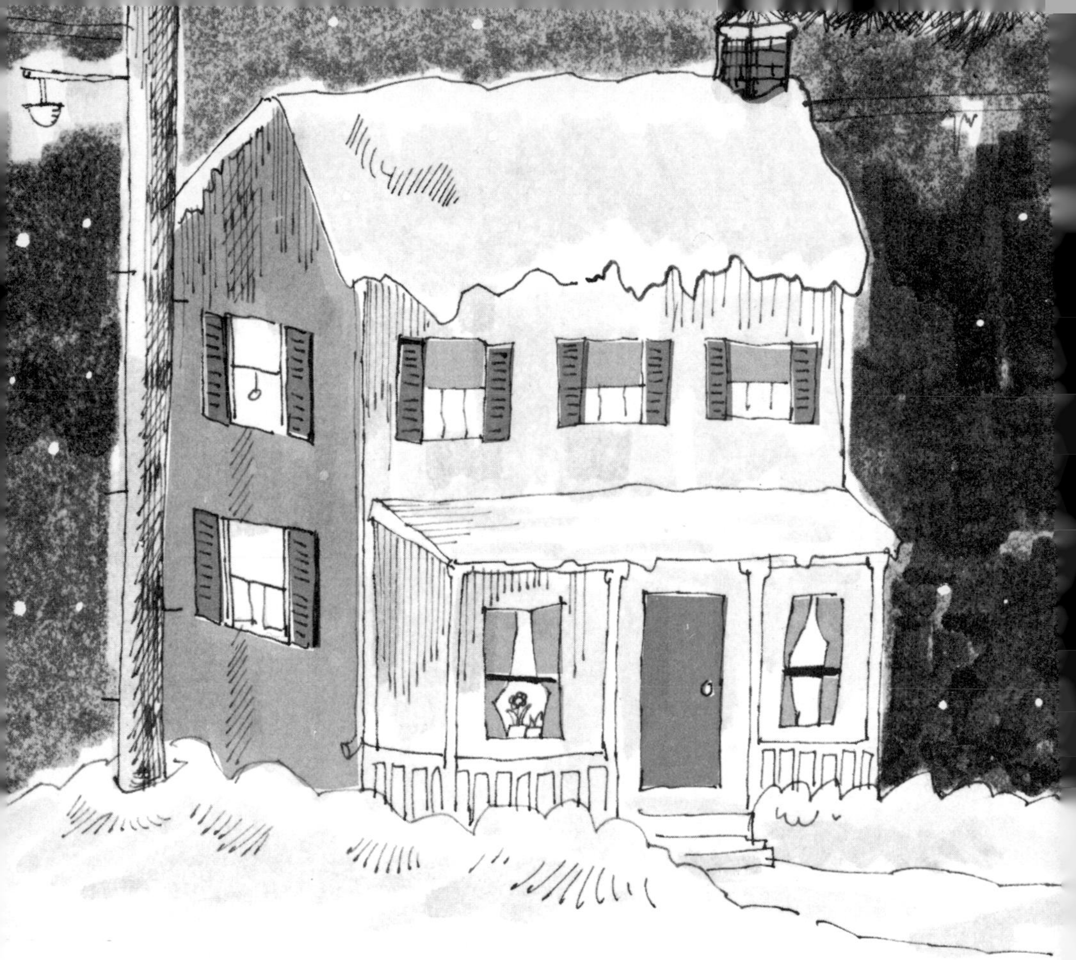

Dinky was chewing on something.

"I did tell you," he said

with his mouth full.

"I said you were wrong about Bobby.

But you never listen to me."

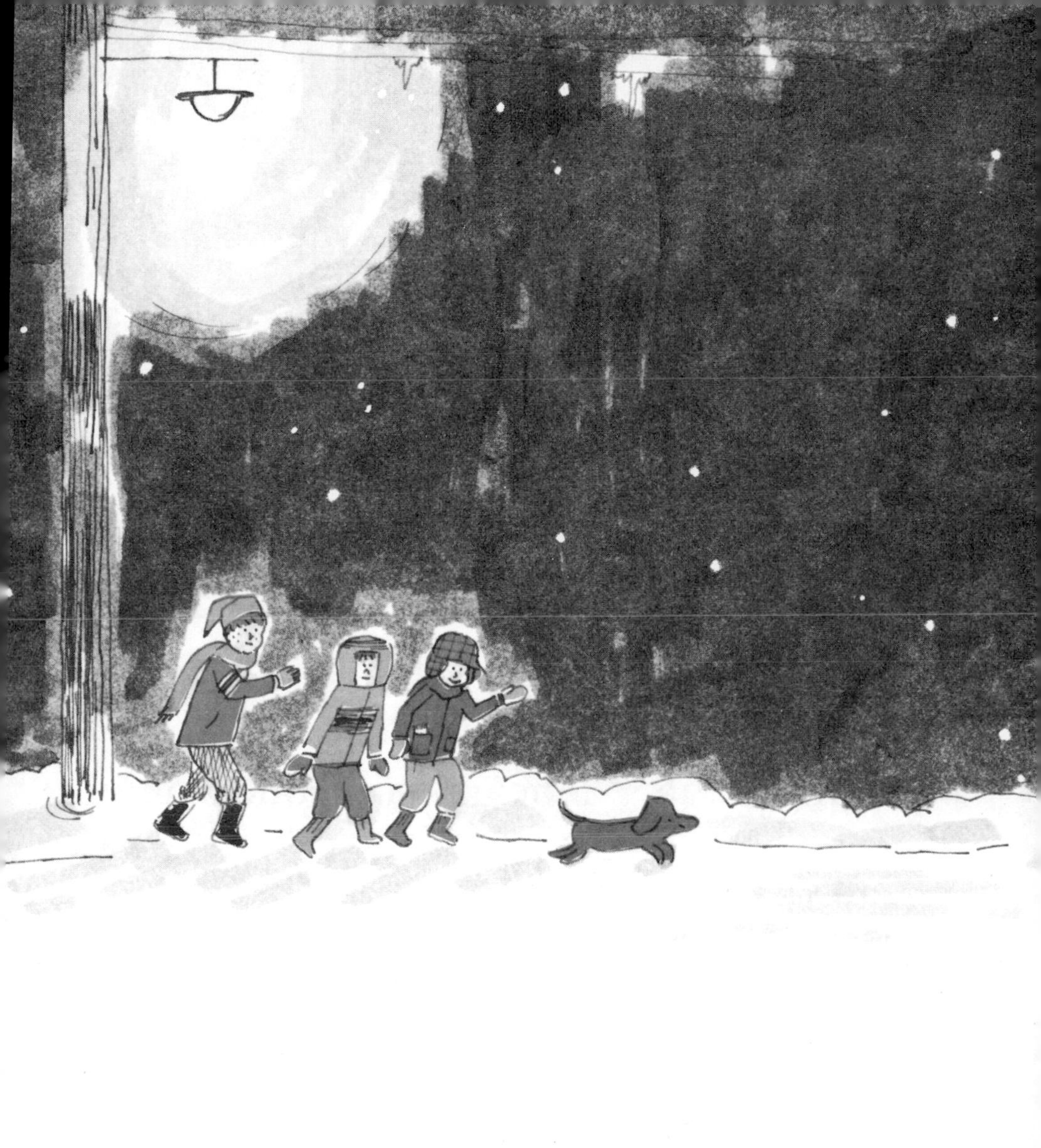

"All right, forget it," said Pinky.
"I will still solve this mystery."
They hurried to the snow fort.

"What happened?" Pinky asked Chub.

"It was too dark to see much,"

said Chub. "I heard someone coming,

and I peeked out.

A big hairy thing jumped on me!

It smashed the whole snow fort.

It took our candy too."

"What a mess!" said Pinky.

"And look at these monster prints!"

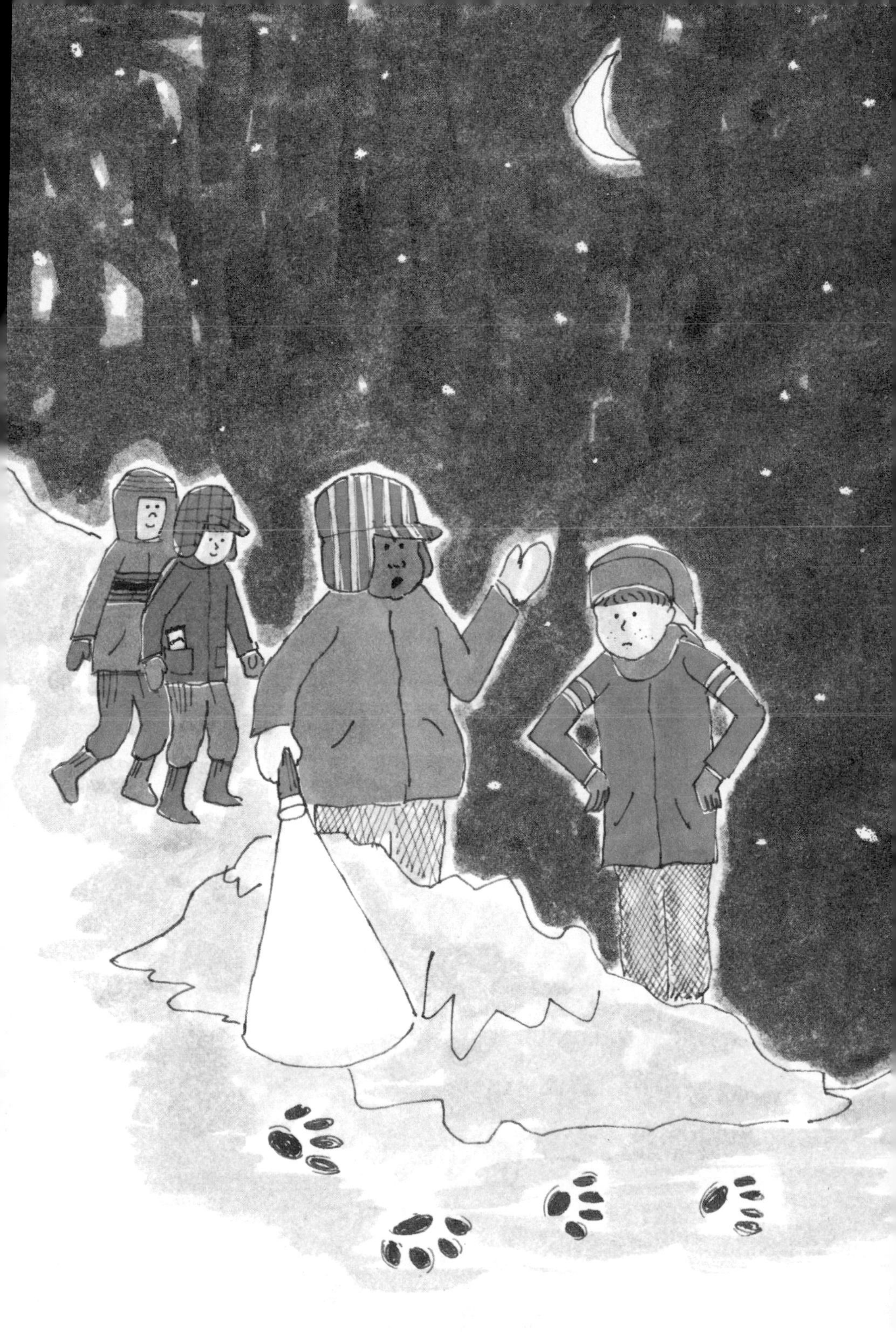

Then Chub saw Bobby.

"Yikes!

What are you doing here?"

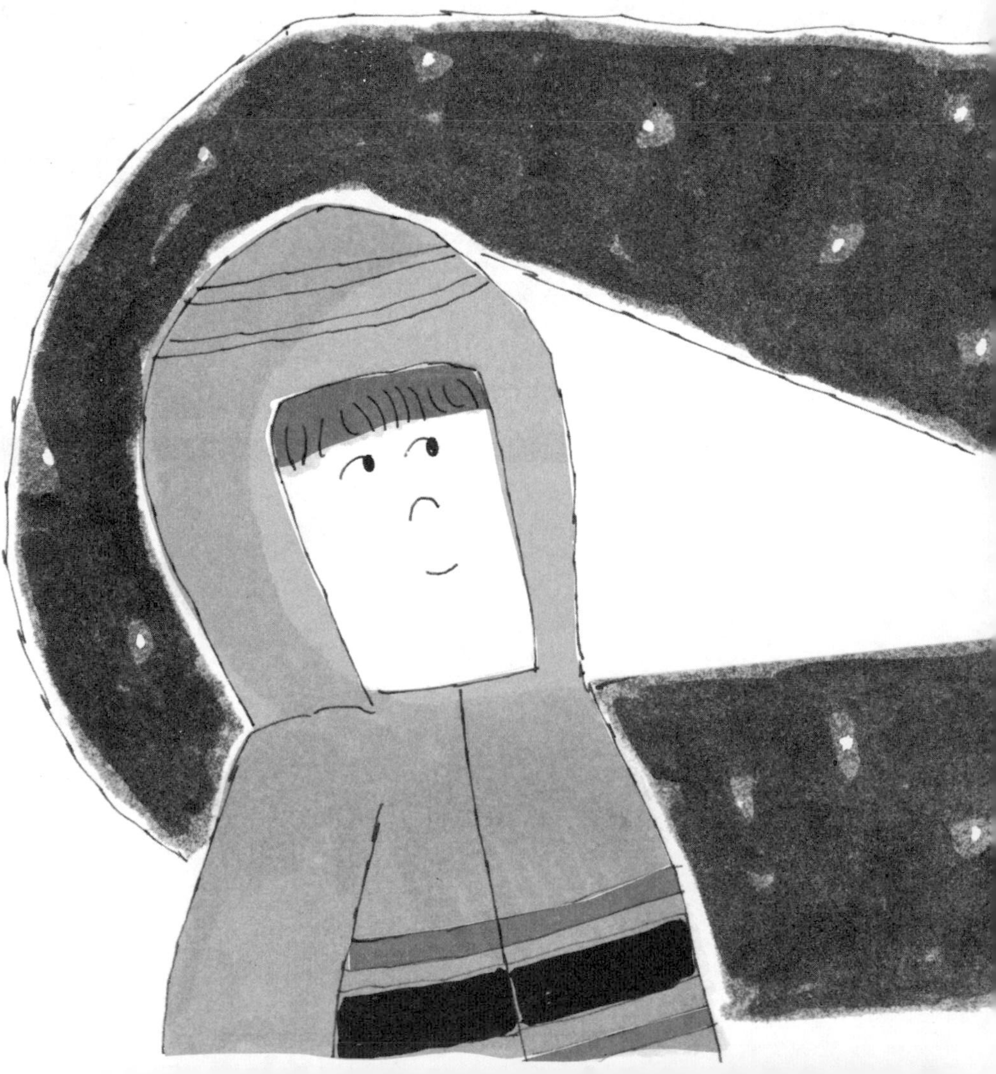

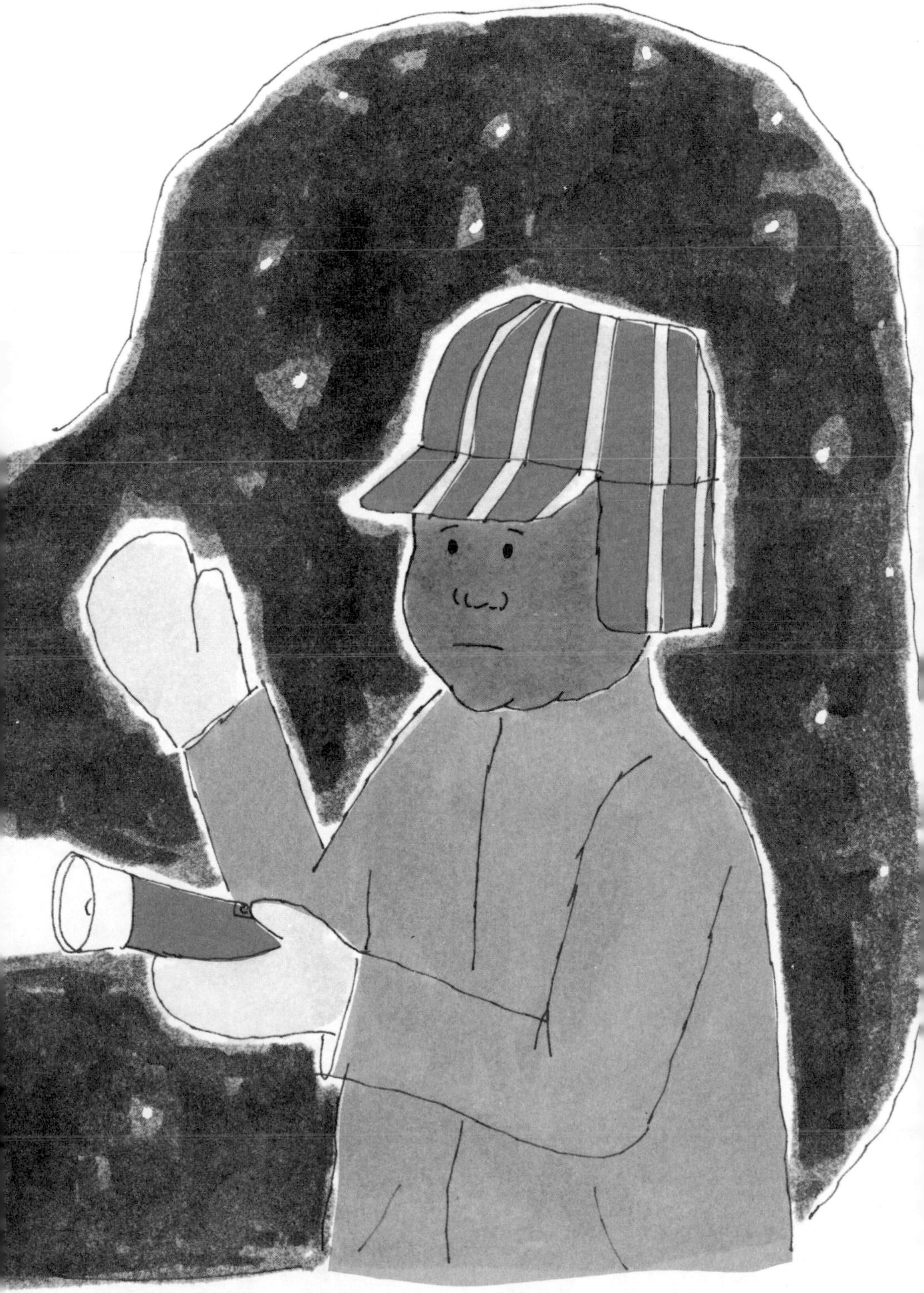

"I came with Dinky," said Bobby.

"But you are the guy I was watching for!" said Chub.

"You are the one who wanted to get in our club."

"I am not," said Bobby.

"Why would I want to get in your dumb old club?
I am a girl."

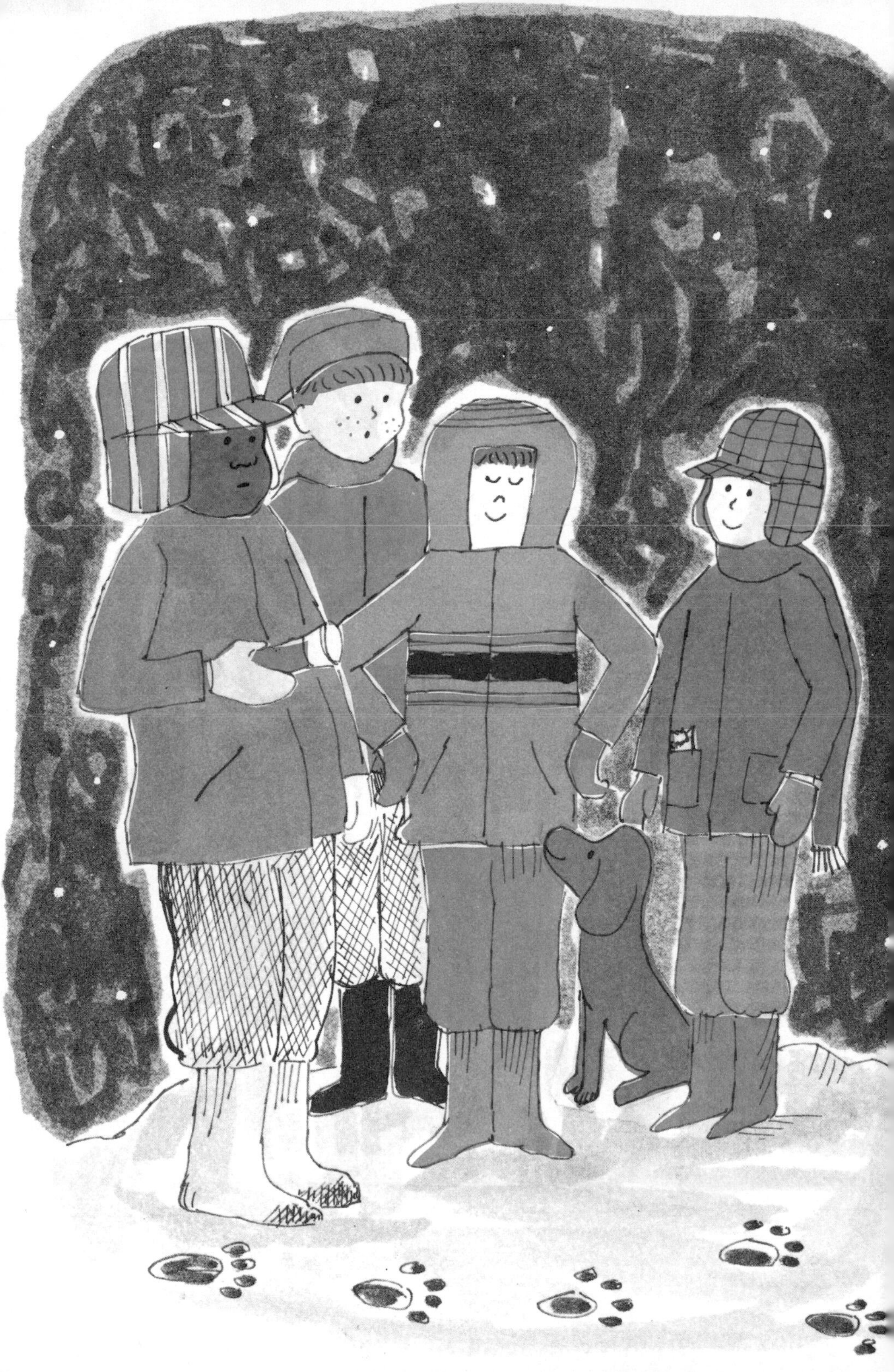

She pulled off her hood.

Pinky and Chub both stared.

"A girl named *Bobby*?" asked Pinky.

Bobby giggled.

"Well, my name is really Roberta.

It is just Bobby for short."

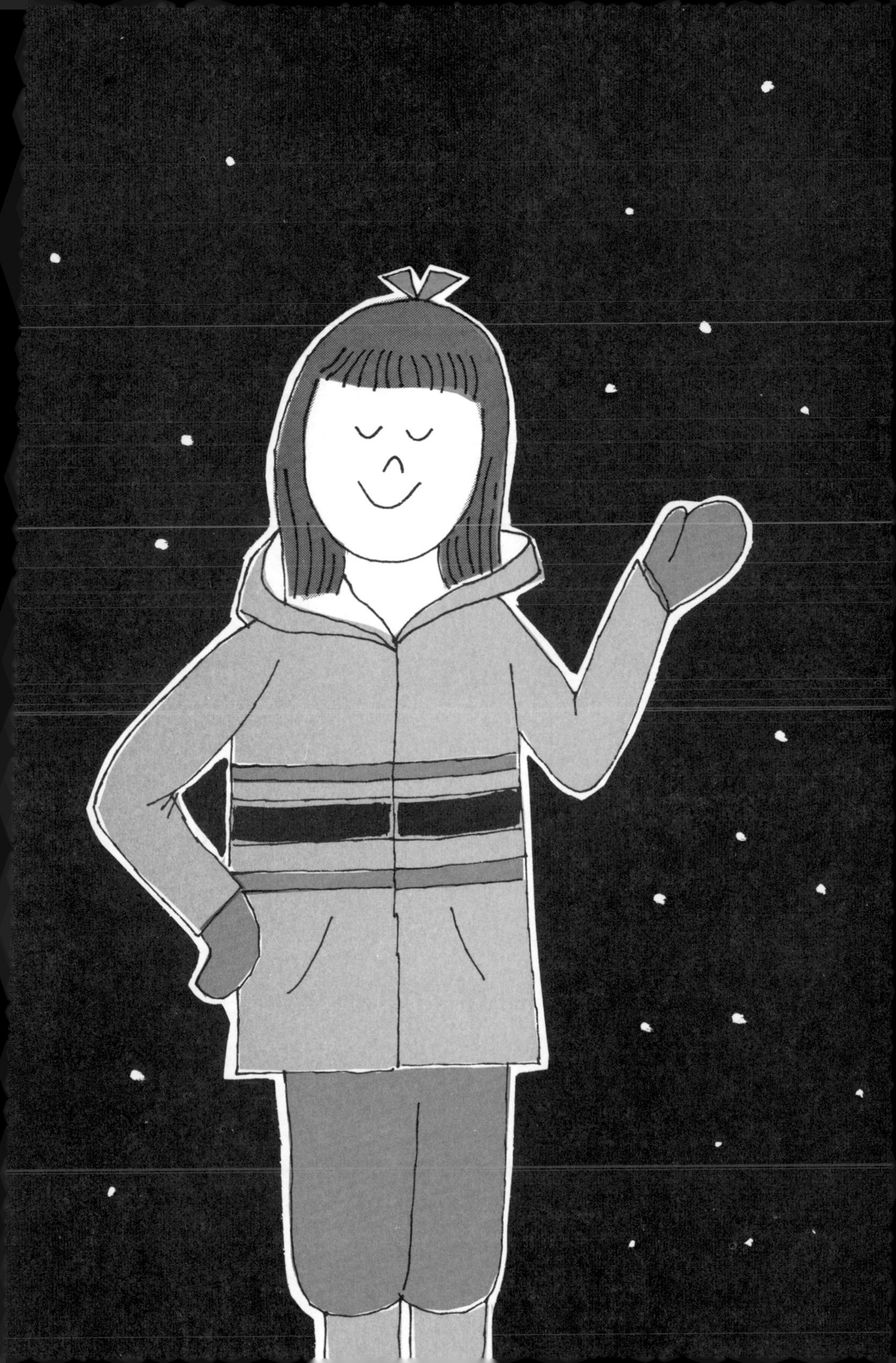

"Would you like to know

who wrecked your snow fort?"

asked Dinky.

"Who?" said Pinky and Chub.

"It will cost you

ten cents each," said Dinky.

Pinky and Chub looked grumpy.

They each gave Dinky a dime.

He gave one to Bobby.

"Okay, who did it?" said Pinky.

"You will see," said Dinky.

47

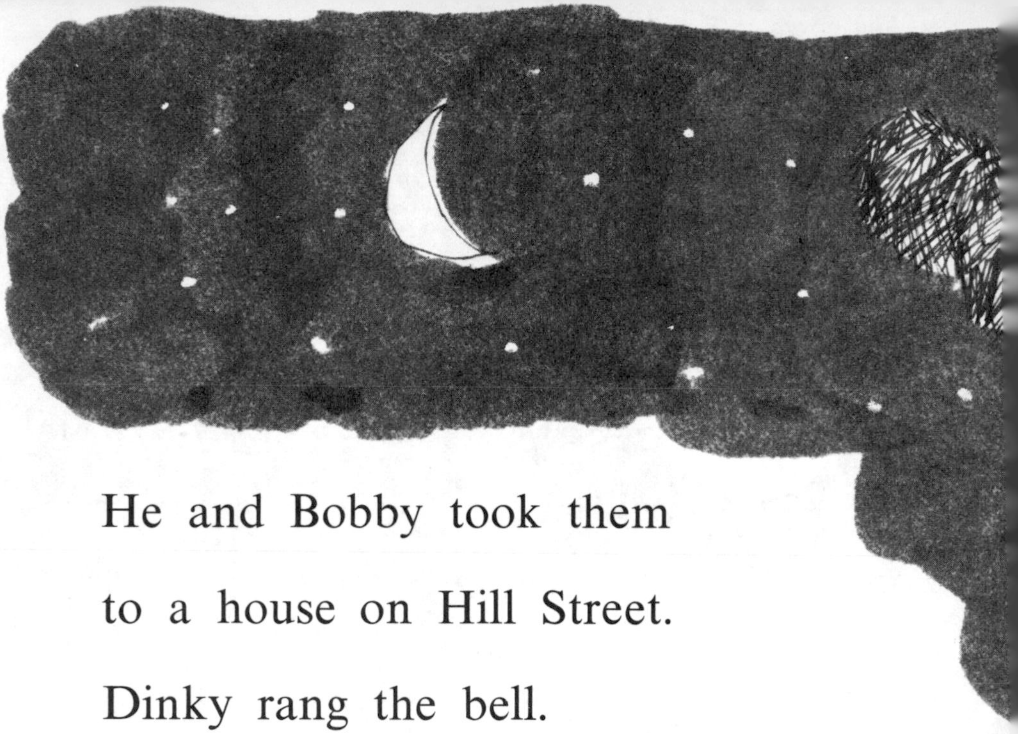

He and Bobby took them
to a house on Hill Street.
Dinky rang the bell.
They heard roars and growls inside.
Pinky and Chub looked scared.
"Don't worry," Bobby said.
"Bozo won't hurt you."

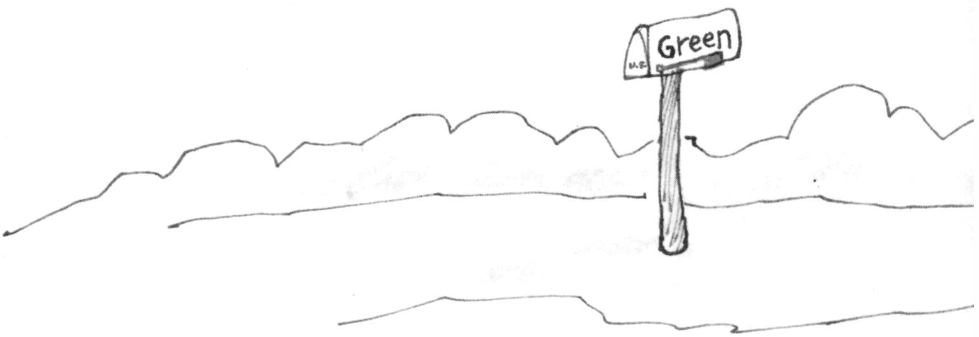
Green

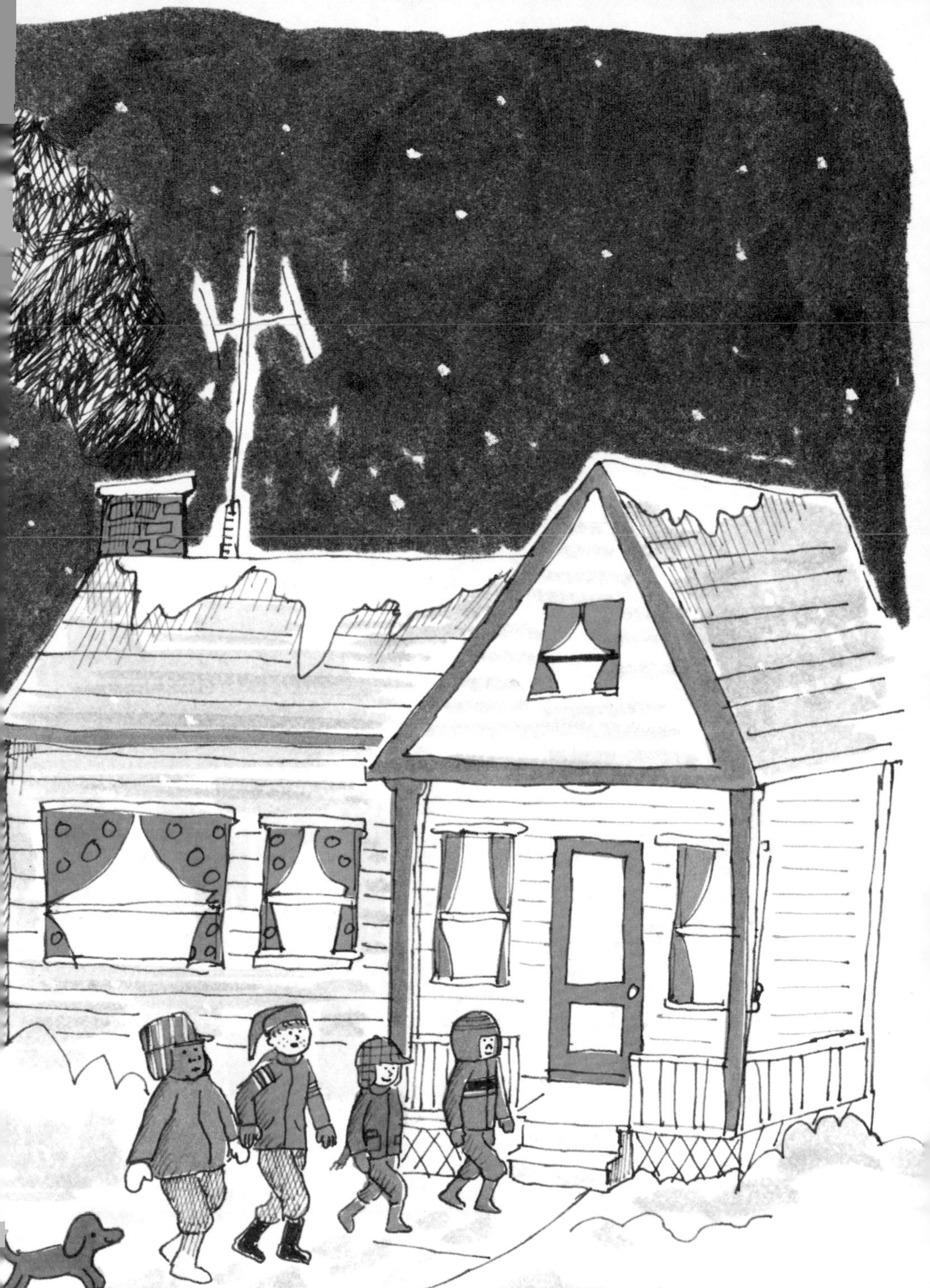

A boy opened the door.

He looked just like Bobby.

A big hairy sheep dog

came jumping out.

The boy pulled him inside.

"Be quiet, Bozo," he said.

"Hey!" said Pinky. "Who are you?"

"He is my brother," said Bobby.

"We are twins.

His name is Robert. Bob for short."

She laughed at the funny look

on Pinky's and Chub's faces.

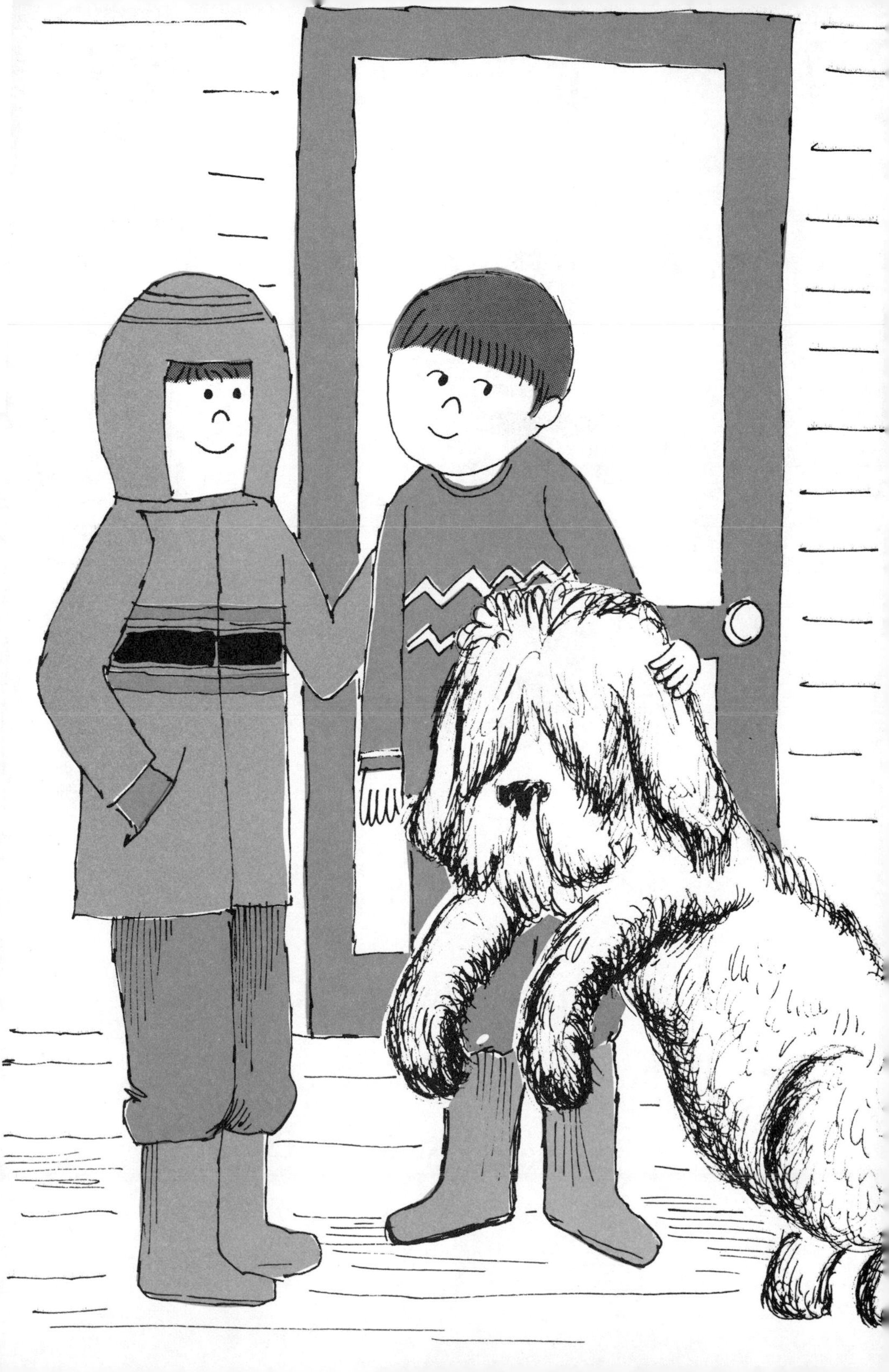

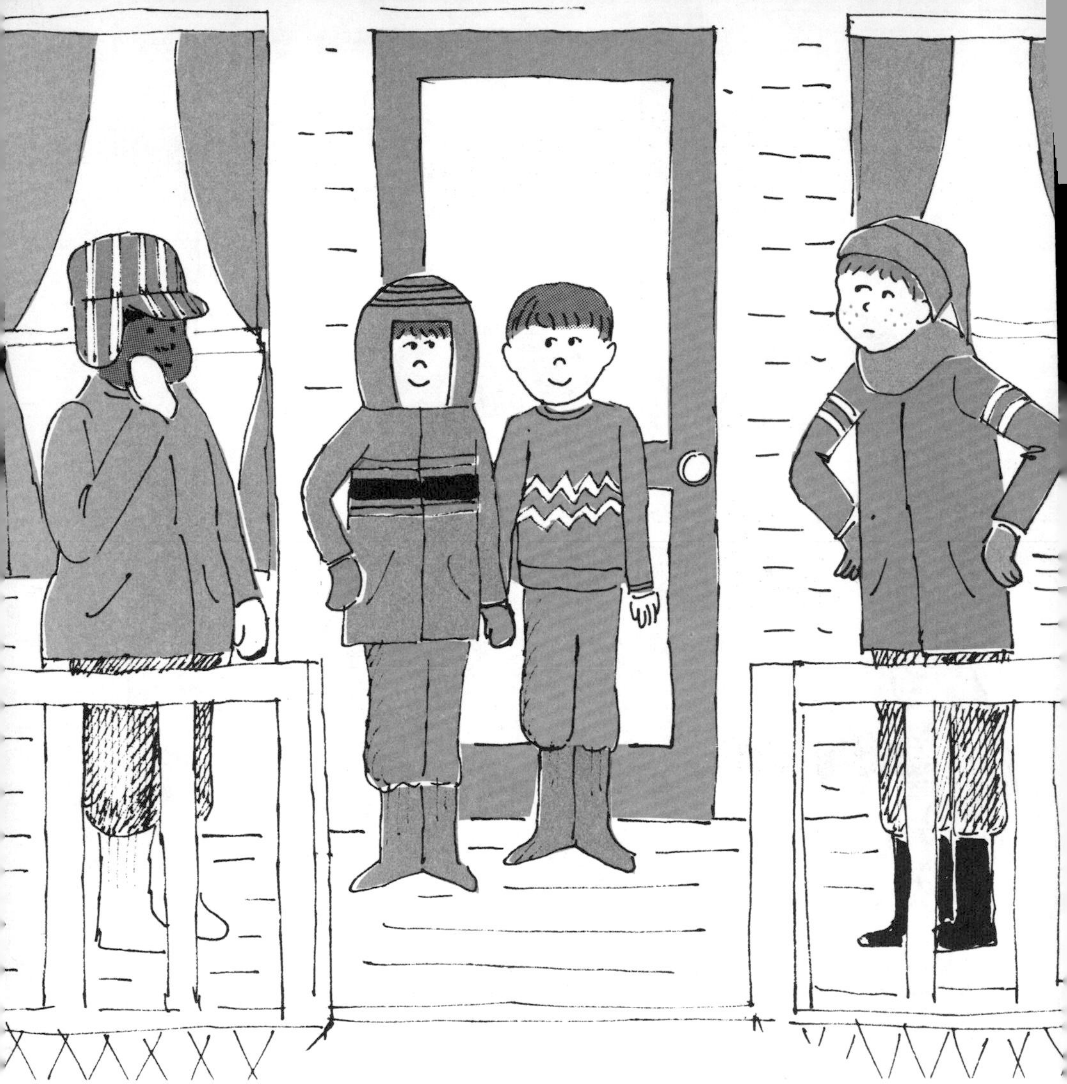

“If you are twins,” said Chub,

“how come you don’t live

in the same house?”

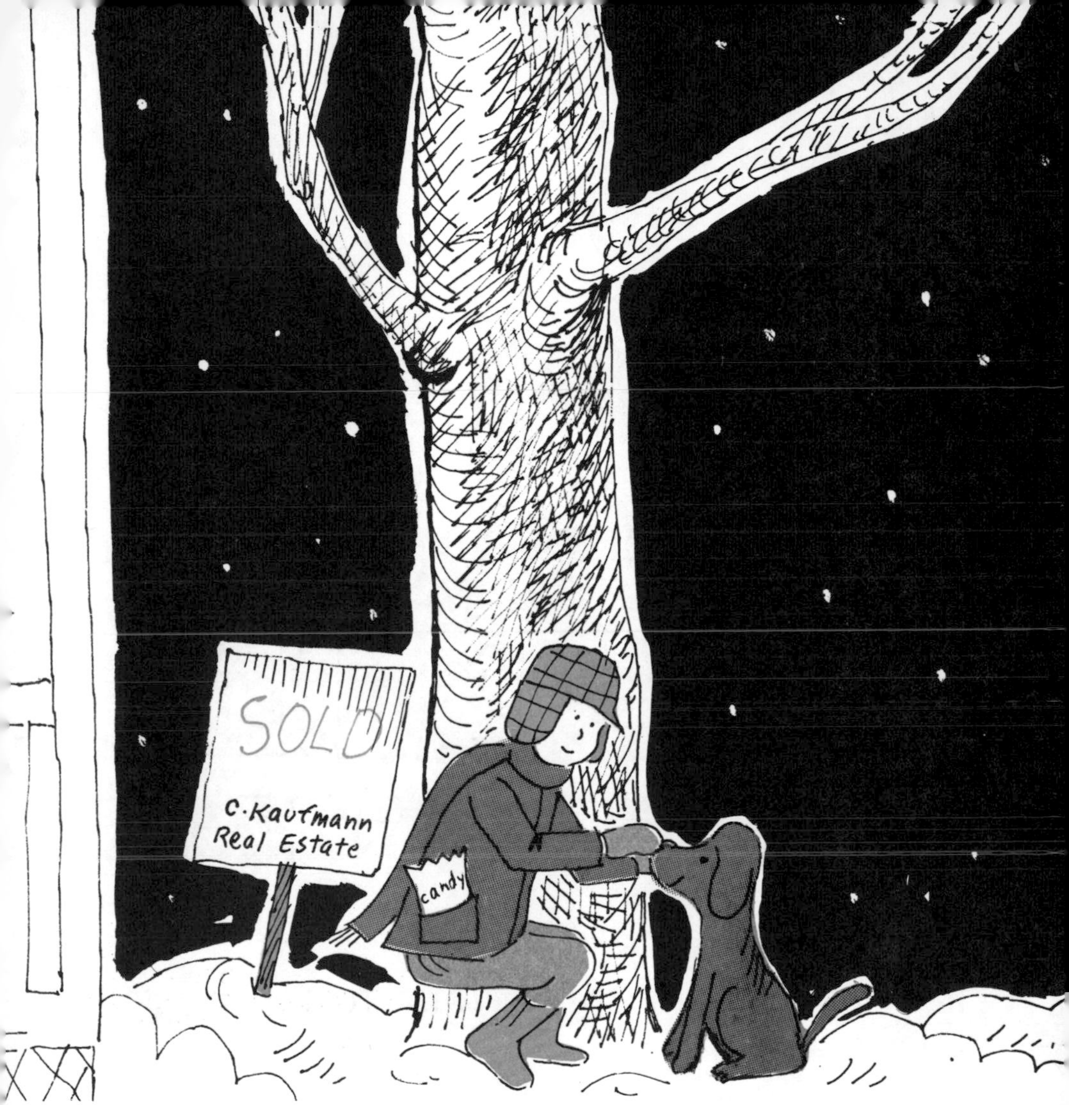
SOLD
C. Kaufmann
Real Estate
candy

"We do," said Bobby.

"This is our *old* house.

We are not done moving yet."

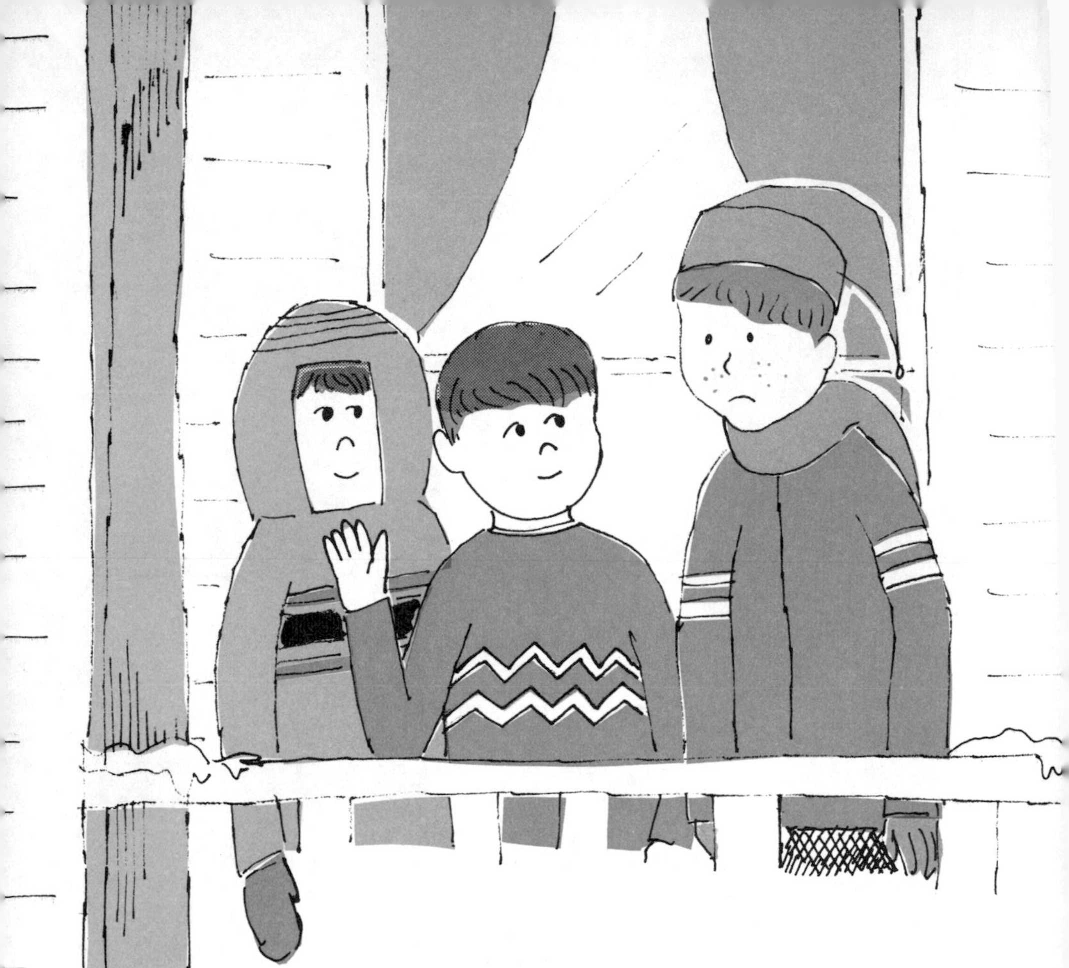

"I am sorry your fort
got wrecked," said Bob.
"I did not really mean
to do anything awful.
That sign was just a joke."

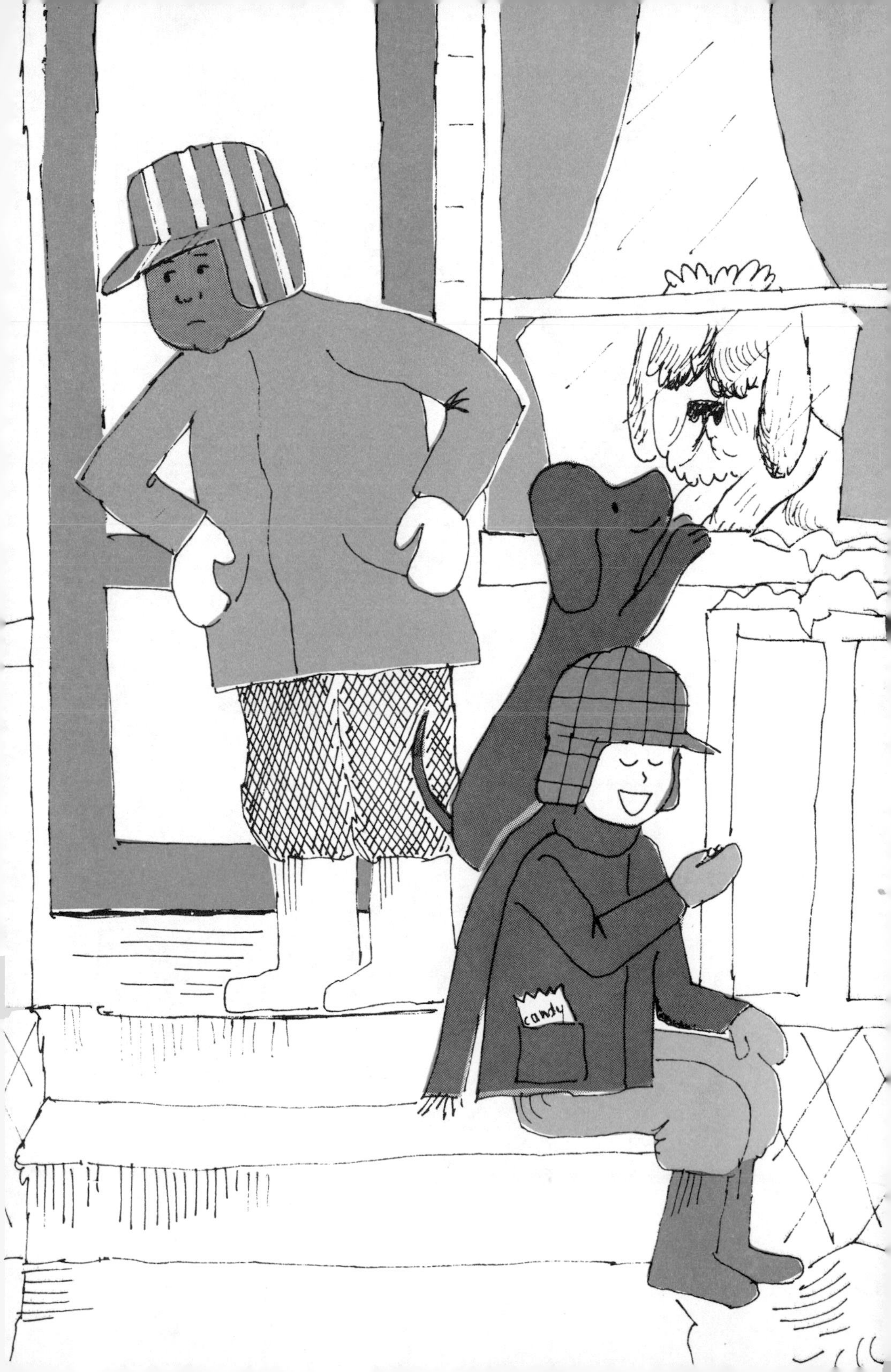
candy

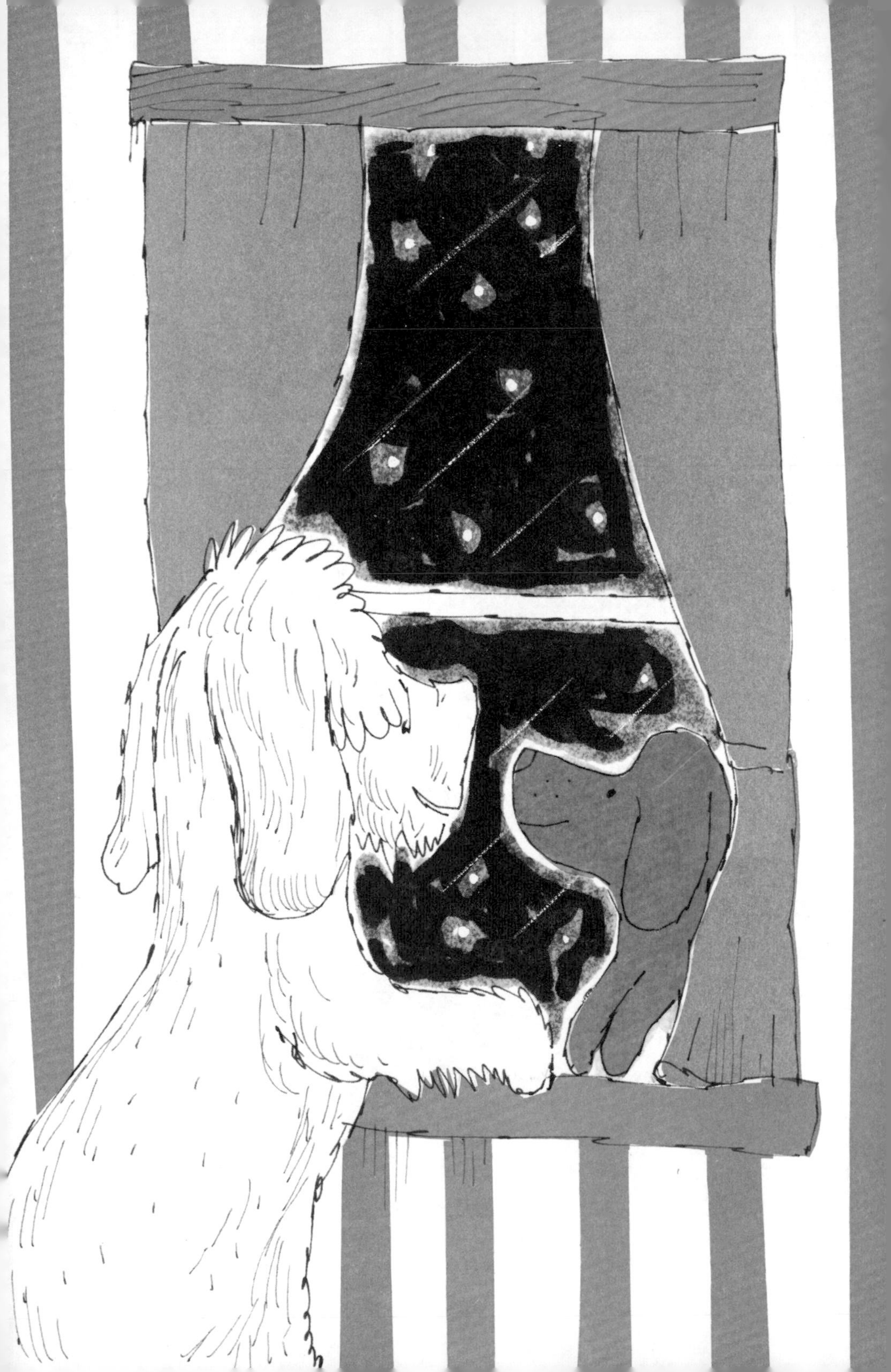

"Very funny," said Pinky.

"If it was only a joke,

how did that awful stuff happen?"

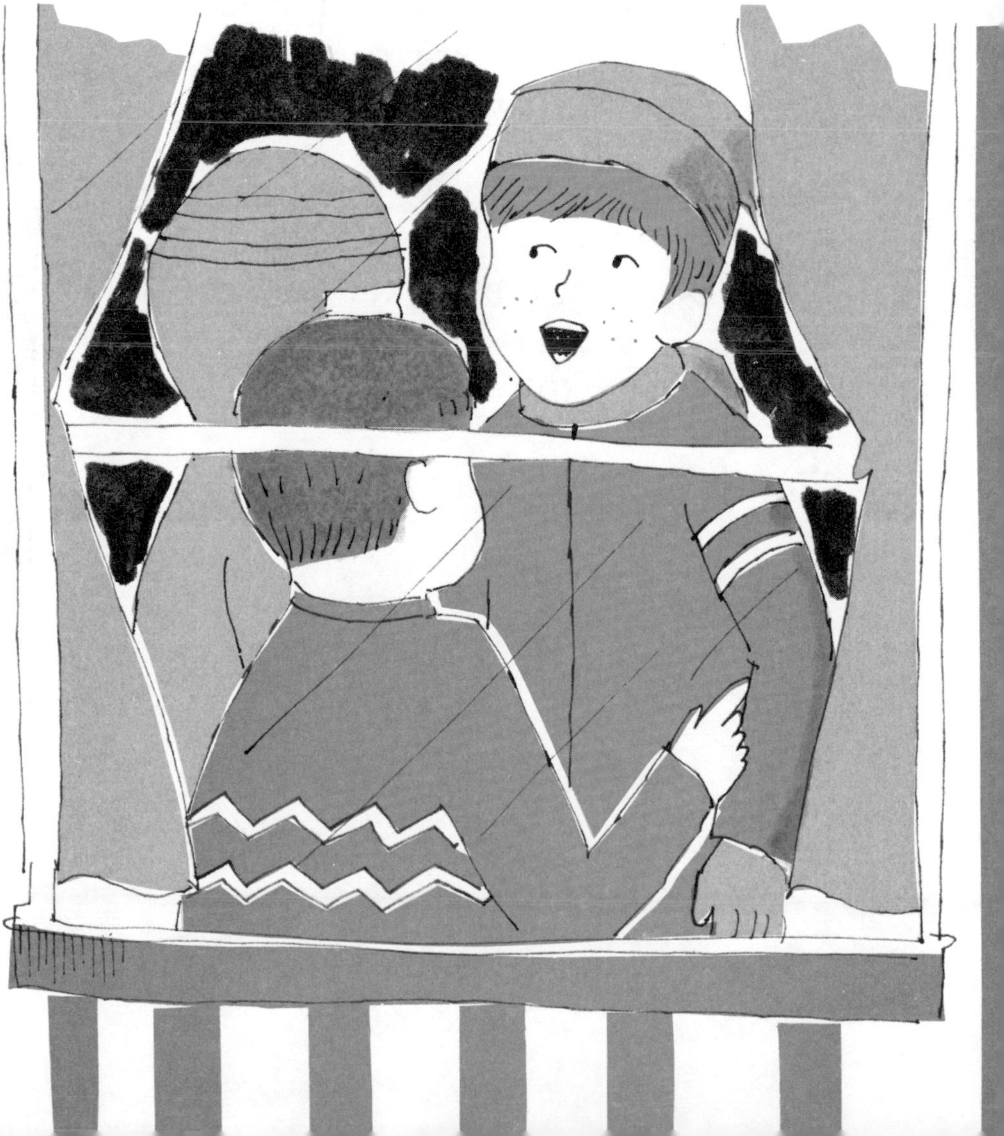

"Well," said Bob,
"I went by your fort again
just to look around.
But someone stuck his head up,
and Bozo got all excited."
"That was my head," said Chub,
"and that big hairy goof
jumped on it."

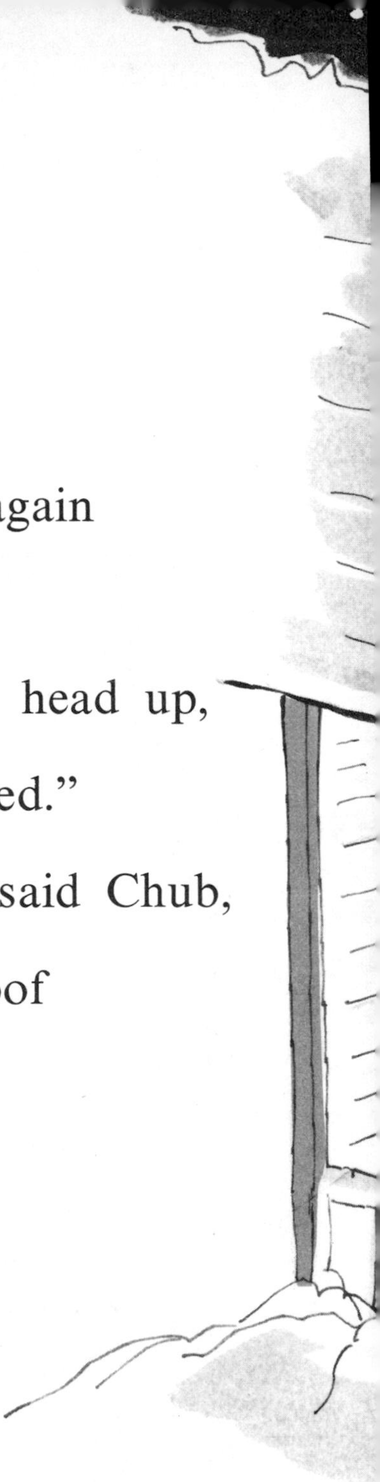

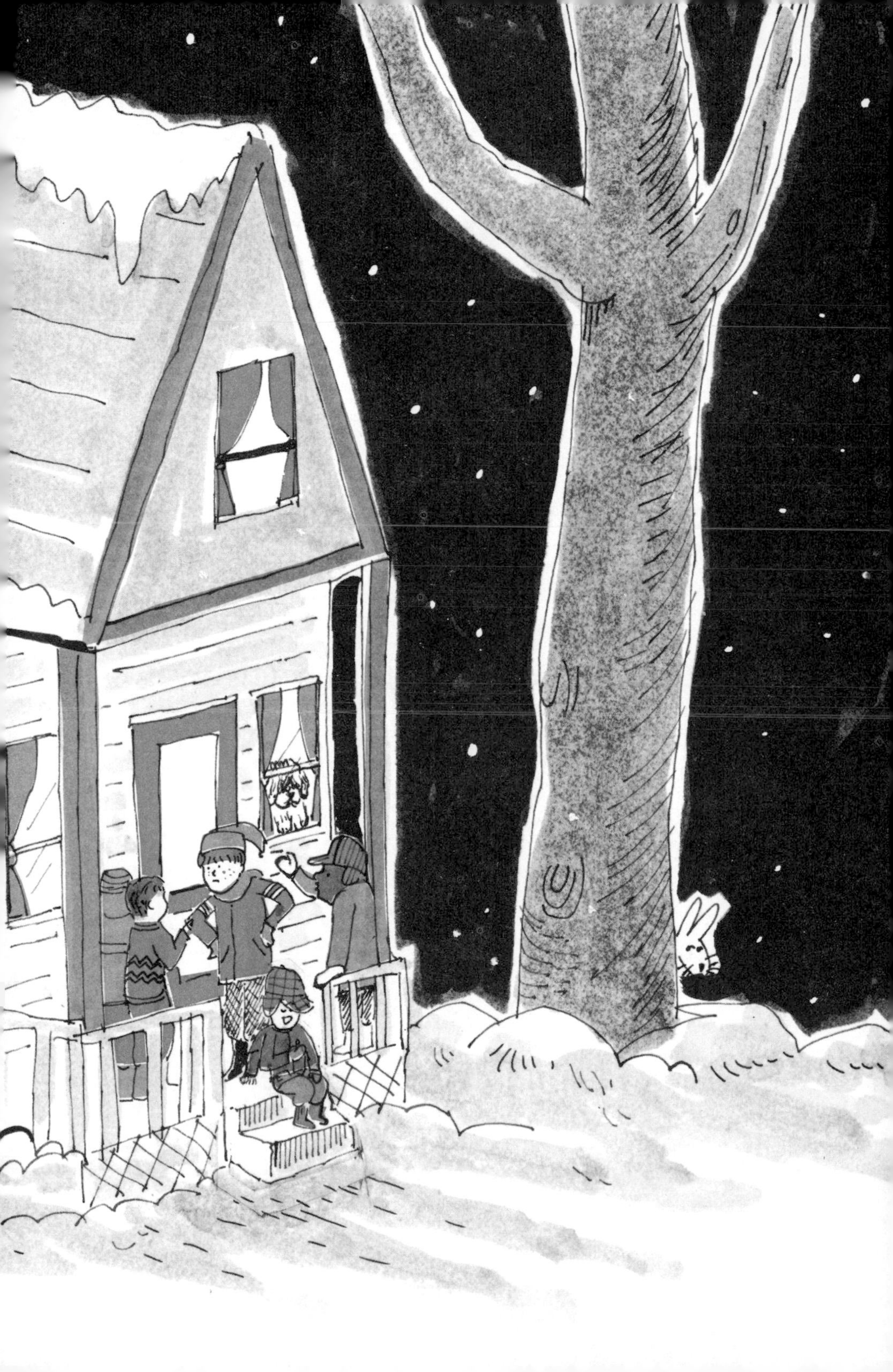

"Bozo is always jumping on things,"
said Bob.

"He is always hungry too.
That is why he took your candy.
And you know what? You were right!"

"Right about what?" asked Pinky.

"About me," said Bob.

"I was afraid you guys would be mad,
so I ran away.
I guess I am not fearless enough."

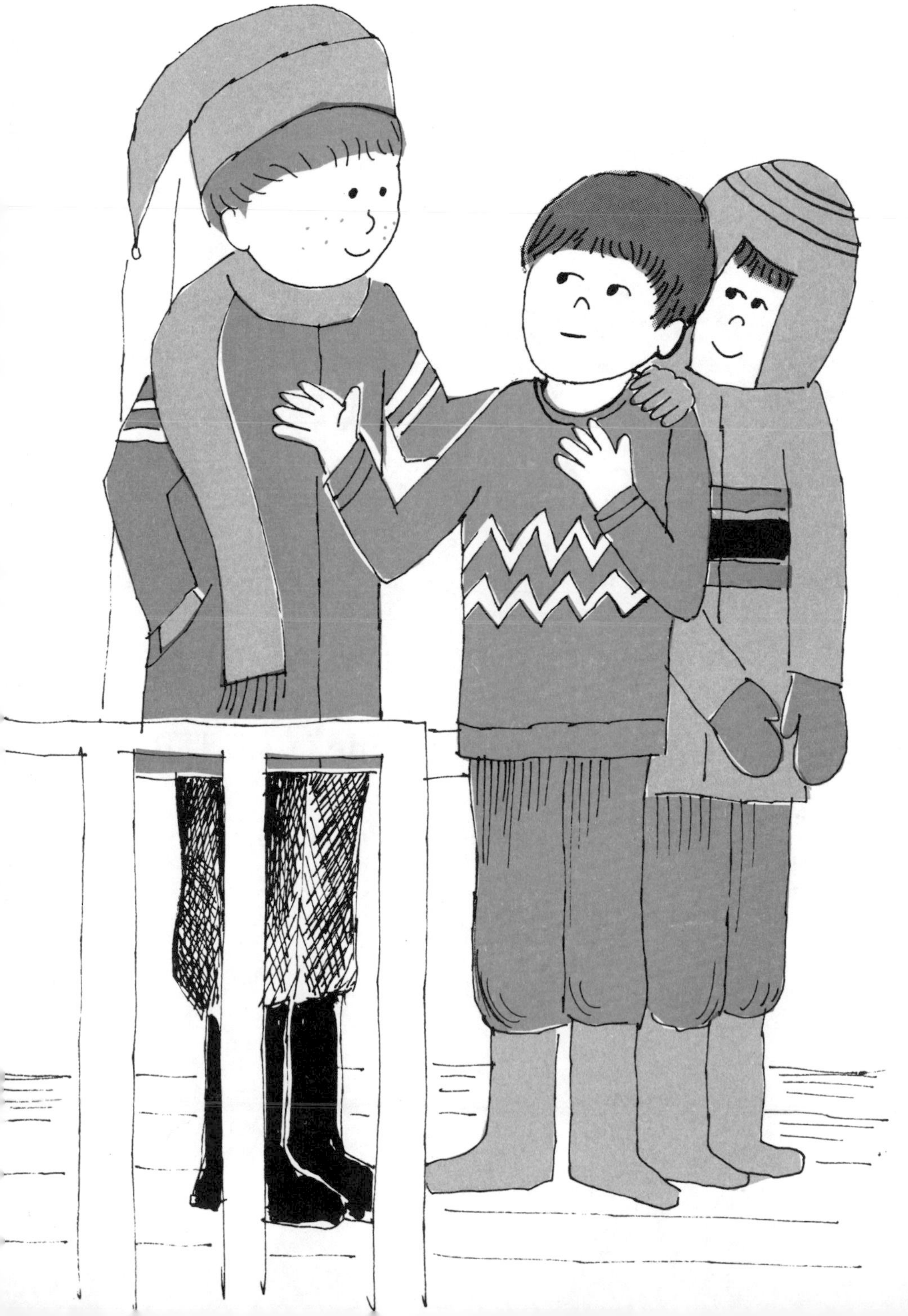

"Never mind," said Chub.

"Where is the candy?"

"It is all gone," said Bob.

"We ate it."

"Who is we?" asked Pinky.

"Well, Bozo and me," said Bob,

"and a couple of others."

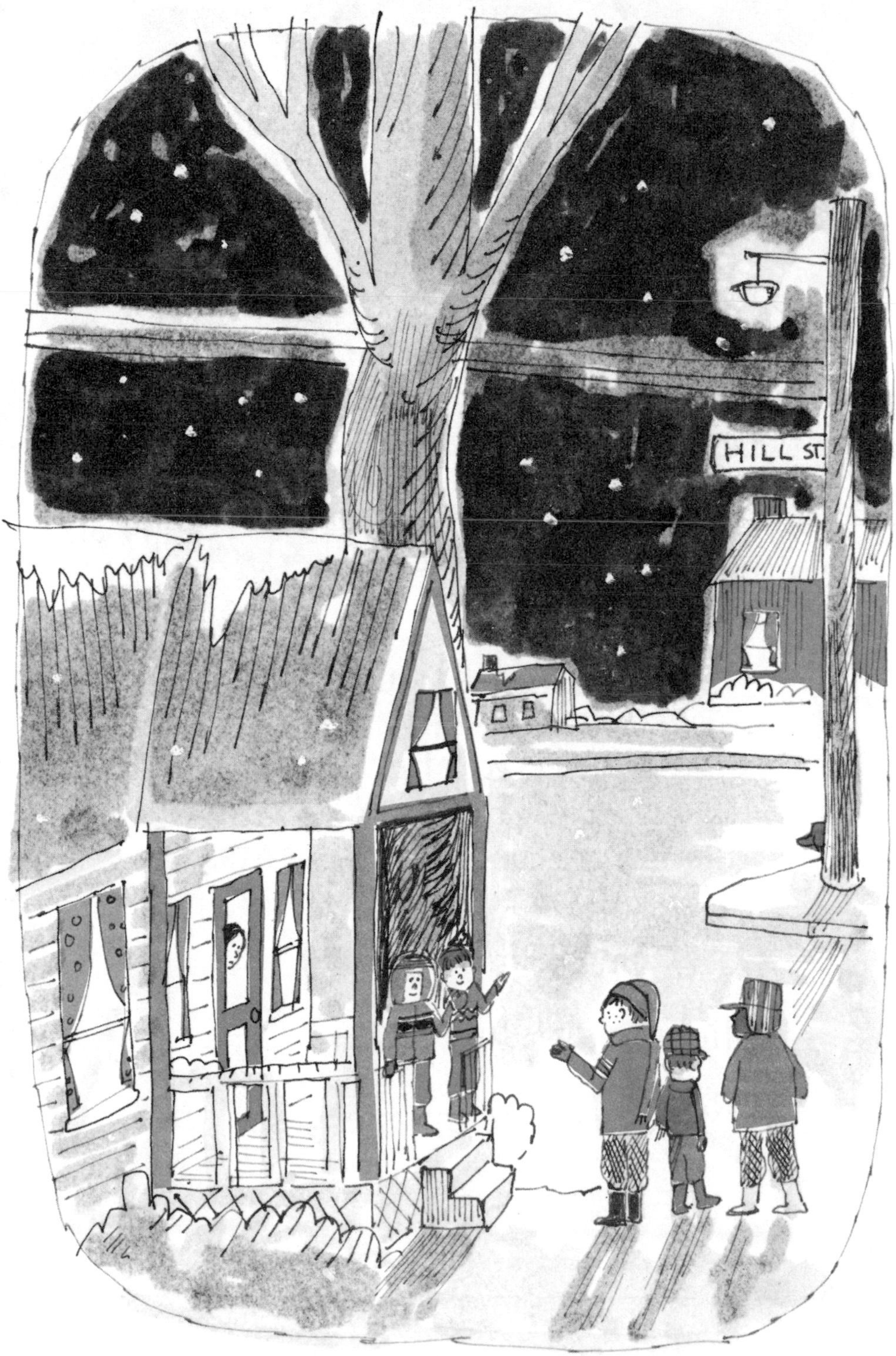
HILL ST.

Pinky glared at his little brother.

"Some nerve," he growled,

"charging us twenty cents."

"So what?" said Dinky,

licking his fingers.

"I solved the mystery for you,

didn't I?"